Honey Bunch AND Norman
AND THE PAPER LANTERN MYSTERY

The HONEY BUNCH AND NORMAN *Series*

By HELEN LOUISE THORNDYKE

———◆●◆———

"What are these funny marks?" Honey Bunch asked

Honey Bunch
AND Norman
AND THE PAPER LANTERN MYSTERY

By
HELEN LOUISE THORNDYKE

NEW YORK
Grosset & Dunlap
PUBLISHERS

CONTENTS

CHAPTER I

TRADING TOYS

"WHEE! See the birdie, Mr. Reilly!" Honey Bunch Morton, age six, cried to her police-dog puppy as she ran around the corner of her house.

"Woof! Woof!" Mr. Reilly replied. Honey Bunch had named her pet after the nice policeman who directed traffic on the next corner.

Honey Bunch's blond hair blew in the breeze and her blue eyes sparkled as she spun on one foot, swinging the toy bird about her head.

Mr. Reilly was jumping up and snapping at the black-and-white paper bird which fluttered at the end of a wire spring.

"Hi, Honey Bunch!" came a call from down the street. It was followed by a clatter and a *bang!*

The little girl looked up just in time to see her playmate, Norman Clark, turn over in his coaster wagon!

1

"Oh, Norman!" she cried, running to the sidewalk. "Are you hurt?"

Norman, who was also six, had played with Honey Bunch ever since he could remember. Now he got up gingerly. "No, I guess I'm all right. My knee is skinned, but it doesn't hurt much."

Back of Norman stood a little boy named Elmer Gray. He was only four.

"I'm awf'lly sorry, Norman," Elmer said.

"It wasn't your fault," Norman said honestly. "I turned the corner too fast!" Then he looked at Honey Bunch and asked, "What's that thing in your hand?"

"A bird. Watch it fly!"

Honey Bunch showed Norman the way the little bird's wings moved up and down when she held up the spring.

The little boy's dark eyes gleamed. "Pollywogs!" he exclaimed. "That's great!" He took the ring on the end of the spring and began to bounce the bird.

"I have something I'll trade you for this," Norman proposed.

Honey Bunch shook her head. Her real name was Gertrude Marian Morton, but no one ever called her that. "No," she said. "Flyer

2

Frank gave the bird to me. Mr. Reilly and I both like it."

Flyer Frank was a young man who had once worked in the law office of Honey Bunch's father. He was now a pilot and often took Honey Bunch and Norman on little trips in his plane. The children were very fond of him.

"Oh, come on," Norman teased. "Mr. Reilly will like what I have, too."

"What is it?"

Norman grinned. "I won't tell you until you give me the spring bird," he insisted.

"I think you should let Honey Bunch guess what it is," Elmer Gray spoke up.

"All right," Norman agreed. "I'll give you five chances, Honey Bunch."

The little girl giggled. She thought a moment, then asked, "Can Mr. Reilly eat it?"

"No, but he might chew it," Norman replied.

"Is it an ear of corn?"

"No, but you could use it on your ear." Norman was enjoying the game.

"It's an ear muff!" Honey Bunch exclaimed.

Norman looked disgusted. "What would Mr. Reilly do with an ear muff?" he said scornfully. "This is something that will make him feel good!"

3

"Is this thing made in the United States?" was Honey Bunch's next question.

Surprised, Norman answered, "No, my daddy says it was made in Japan."

"Where's Japan?" Elmer wanted to know.

"It's a long way from here," Honey Bunch replied. "Flyer Frank says it's just about as far away as you can get and if you go any farther you're on your way home!"

"That's silly!" Norman remarked. "How could you be on your way home if you're going to Japan?"

"I don't know," Honey Bunch admitted. "Anyway, Flyer Frank brought the bird from there. He said the bus drivers had toys like this hanging from the ceiling of their buses."

"I'd like to ride in that kind of a bus," Elmer said wistfully.

"And in Japan," Honey Bunch went on, "Flyer Frank says some of the little girls wear flowered kimonos and carry pretty parasols."

But Norman was not interested in what little girls in Japan wore. "Oh, come on, Honey Bunch," he pleaded. "If your bird came from Japan and my present did, too, why won't you trade?"

Honey Bunch gave in. "All right, Norman, if you think Mr. Reilly will like it."

4

A board fence separated the Clarks' yard from the Mortons' property. Norman ran to the fence and scrambled over it.

Just then, Elmer's mother called him to come home. Honey Bunch walked with her little friend around to the Mortons' front yard. She promised to show Elmer her exchange gift later.

In a few minutes Norman was back, holding something behind him.

"Did you get it?" Honey Bunch asked eagerly.

"Yes. Here it is." Norman held out a long carved stick. On one end were what looked like tiny fingers.

Honey Bunch's smile faded. "Wh-what is it?" she asked, trying not to show her disappointment.

"A Japanese back-scratcher!" Norman cried triumphantly.

"But how can Mr. Reilly use that?" the little girl wailed.

Norman rumpled his black hair. "Pollywogs! It's easy. Watch!"

He took the back-scratcher and gently ran it along the puppy's back. Mr. Reilly squirmed in delight. When Norman stopped, the puppy stood up on his hind legs and begged for more.

While the children were playing with Mr.

Reilly, a young man had been watching from the other side of the street. Now he crossed over and came up to them.

The blond stranger was of medium height, with narrow shoulders and a thin face.

"Hi, kids!" he said, nervously blinking his pale-blue eyes.

Honey Bunch and Norman answered hello.

"Do you two live in this neighborhood?" the man asked, taking a notebook from his pocket.

"This is Honey Bunch's house," Norman replied, "and my house is on the next street."

6

"I'm looking for a Japanese family. Do you know any around here?" the stranger went on.

"You mean real Japanese people?" Honey Bunch inquired. "Ones who wear kimonos and carry parasols?"

The man laughed. "I don't think they'd be wearing kimonos in the United States, but they did come here from Japan."

"I haven't seen anybody like that around here," Honey Bunch said.

Norman spoke up. "I saw a Japanese man downtown the other day," he volunteered. "At least my daddy said he was. He was in the drugstore when Daddy and I were there and they started talking about Japan."

"You don't know where he lives?" the stranger asked.

Norman shook his head. "Why are you looking for him?"

The stranger did not answer the question. He said good-by and went down the street.

"He acted funny, didn't he, Norman?" Honey Bunch said, as the man turned the corner and disappeared.

"Yes, kind of," Norman agreed.

"Honey Bunch! Honey Bunch!" came a call from the back door of the Mortons' house.

7

"That's Mrs. Miller," the little girl said. "Let's see what she wants."

"Maybe she has some cookies," Norman guessed hopefully.

Mrs. Miller was the pleasant woman who had helped Mrs. Morton with the housework ever since Honey Bunch was a baby. All the children in the neighborhood loved the delicious cookies she baked.

Now Honey Bunch and Norman ran around the side of the house. Norman had the ring at the end of the spring on his finger. The little black-and-white bird's wings flapped wildly.

"Would you children like some cookies and milk?" Mrs. Miller asked them when they reached the kitchen door.

"Oh, how scrumptious!" Honey Bunch exclaimed.

"Yum!" Norman said. "Chocolate cookies!"

Mrs. Miller noticed the bird bobbing from Norman's hand. "Isn't that the bird Flyer Frank gave you, Honey Bunch?" she asked.

Honey Bunch said it was. "But I traded it for this Japanese back-scratcher," she explained, showing her new possession. "Mr. Reilly likes to have his back scratched!"

8

"I think, Norman, you'd better give the bird back to Honey Bunch."

The little boy looked downcast, but replied, "All right, Mrs. Miller, after I play with it just once more!"

Mrs. Miller gave each of the children a paper plate with a glass of milk and two large chocolate cookies. "Why don't you eat them over there under the apple tree?" she suggested.

"All right," said Honey Bunch.

The children walked over and sat down on the grass in the shade of the leafy branches. Honey Bunch's beautiful black cat, Lady Clare, came by. She carried her head high to show off the fluffy white fur which formed a collar around her neck.

Norman called, "Here, kitty, kitty! Have something good." He held out a piece of his cookie.

But Norman sometimes teased Lady Clare. So she turned her back on him and climbed up the tree, where she crouched on a low branch.

When the children had finished the cookies and milk, Norman stood up.

"May I make the bird fly now, Honey Bunch?" he asked.

His playmate agreed and Norman began to

run around the yard pulling the toy through the air. As he ran the little bird flew up and down, its wings fluttering in the breeze.

"Oh boy! This is fun!" Norman cried.

"Watch out!" Honey Bunch warned.

Her playmate had run under the branch of the apple tree where Lady Clare crouched. With a mighty spring the cat leaped at the bird. She landed on the grass, her mouth full of feathers!

CHAPTER II

TOO MANY LANTERNS

"NORMAN!" Honey Bunch screamed, "Lady Clare has my bird!"

Norman turned quickly. He chased the cat away and stooped to pick up the paper bird. But all that remained were the two black-and-white wings! The rest of the feathered toy was scattered on the grass in tiny pieces!

Poor Norman! He was always getting into trouble. But he could be a big help, too—especially when he and Honey Bunch found little mysteries to solve, like *The Pine Cone Mystery*.

"I'm sorry," Norman apologized. "I guess Lady Clare thought it was a real bird."

"What's all the excitement about?" The question came from a slender, dark-haired woman who was peering over the fence.

"I was making Honey Bunch's paper bird fly, Mother," Norman explained. "Lady Clare thought it was real and tried to eat it!"

11

"My bird came all the way from Japan," Honey Bunch remarked sadly.

"Don't feel bad," Mrs. Clark said consolingly. "Norman will get you another bird. I just saw a new Japanese store downtown. It's called The Tokyo Shop and is opening today. I'm sure they will have some paper birds."

"A Japanese shop!" Honey Bunch exclaimed. "Norman, do you suppose the Japanese man you and your daddy saw owns the store?"

"Maybe! And perhaps he's the one that American man was looking for a little while ago!"

Mrs. Clark looked puzzled. The children told her about the strange man with the blinking eyes who had talked to them. After Mrs. Clark left the fence, Mrs. Miller came outside and asked the children if they would like to go for a walk downtown with her.

"Would we!" Norman exclaimed. Then he added, "Mrs. Miller, could we go to the new Japanese shop so I can buy another bird for Honey Bunch? Lady Clare ruined the other one."

"I guess we can," Mrs. Miller agreed, "that is if your mother approves."

Honey Bunch clapped her hands. "Oh,
12

thank you, Mrs. Miller. Let's go right now!"

Norman ran home to ask permission and get
some money to buy the bird. When he came
back, the three started out for the shopping area
of Barham where they lived. It was only a
short distance from the Morton's home.

They reached The Tokyo Shop and went in.
"Isn't it pretty!" Honey Bunch cried, looking
around.

On the walls hung long pictures which Mrs.
Miller called scrolls. The display tables
around the edge of the room were covered with
colorful tea sets and bowls of black or red lac-
quer.

At the moment there were no other customers
in the shop. A slender man of medium height
with straight black hair came up to greet them.

"Good afternoon," he said in a pleasant voice
with a slight accent. "I am Taki Kito. Welcome to The Tokyo Shop."

Norman replied, "I saw you the other day in
the drugstore. You talked to my daddy."

The Japanese smiled. "Ah yes, I remember.
Mr. Clark. I had a very interesting discussion
with your father."

Honey Bunch and Norman described the
black-and-white bird that Lady Clare had

13

"Oh, aren't they darling!" Honey Bunch exclaimed

ruined. "I want to buy one like it for **Honey Bunch**," Norman explained.

Mr. Kito bowed. "I am so sorry. I do not have one just now. Many of my things are still unpacked. But if you can wait a day or two I will have a bird for you."

Honey Bunch said that would be all right. Just then she saw a collection of tiny Japanese dolls. "Oh, aren't they darling!" she exclaimed, running over to admire the little figures.

Norman paused to examine a table of Japanese flower arrangements. He picked up a white box to look at the queer black markings on it. As he did so, the top slipped off and the bottom fell out.

Clatter, clatter! Hundreds of small, black stones cascaded to the floor and scattered in all directions.

"Pollywogs! I'm sorry!" Norman apologized, dropping to his knees and beginning to pick up the shiny stones.

"No harm done," Mr. Kito replied. "I have children myself and know how hard it is for them to keep from touching things!"

Honey Bunch ran over to help and in a few minutes the children had collected all the stones and put them back in the white box.

Next they inspected a tank of Japanese gold-fish near the front of the store. "They're pretty," Honey Bunch said. "May I buy this one, Mrs. Miller?" She pointed to a fish which had a beautiful feathery tail and fins. Mrs. Miller nodded.

"Ah yes," Mr. Kito said as he lifted the fish from the tank with a little net and dropped it into a small glass bowl. "This one is a lady fish. You can tell by the mild expression on her face!"

The children giggled as Mrs. Miller paid for the goldfish. They were starting to leave when Mr. Kito called:

"Here are my children now. I would like you to meet them!"

From behind the screen at the back of the shop came two small figures. Both had shiny black hair and sparkling brown eyes.

"This is my daughter Aniko," Mr. Kito explained. "She is seven and her brother Nikkio is six." Both children bowed solemnly from the waist.

Honey Bunch curtsied and Norman bowed, then Norman said to the little boy, "You're the same age as Honey Bunch and me. May we call you Nick?"

The little Japanese boy grinned shyly in agreement, then turned to his father. "Aniko and I have come to help you unpack," he said.

"Thank you," the Japanese man replied. "The cartons are in the back. I will be with you in a minute."

"Norman and I love to open packages," Honey Bunch spoke up. "Could we please help you unpack some of your things?"

"Yes," Norman agreed. "Maybe we could find the box with the paper birds in it!"

Mrs. Miller started to refuse, but Mr. Kito, smiling at her, said, "That would be very helpful if you would allow it."

Finally Mrs. Miller consented. She said she had some shopping to do and would return for the children in an hour.

Honey Bunch and Norman followed the Japanese children to the rear of the shop where many large packing boxes were stacked. Aniko went over to one which stood by itself on the floor. It was full of shredded paper.

"There are dishes in here," Aniko explained. "We'll take them all out so they can be washed."

The four children set to work eagerly and carefully lifted plates and cups and saucers from the wooden box. As they were unwrapped,

Honey Bunch sorted them into sets on a nearby table.

"That is finished," Nikkio said presently, and began to drag the box toward the back door.

"Wait a minute," Honey Bunch called. "We haven't unpacked all the dishes."

"Sure we have," Norman told her, coming over to examine the china on the table.

"But there are only five of each thing instead of six!" Honey Bunch pointed out.

Aniko and Nikkio began to laugh. Then, seeing the puzzled expressions on the other children's faces, Aniko explained. "There are supposed to be five. Japanese do not like even numbers. We think they are unlucky, so we make all things in sets of five or seven or nine or eleven."

Norman chuckled. "Then Nick, Honey Bunch, and I should be five years old instead of six. We're unlucky the age we are!"

"But we'll be lucky again when we're seven!" Honey Bunch giggled.

At this point Mr. Kito came into the room. "I need some paper lanterns to put in the window tonight," he said. "Have you seen a carton marked 'lanterns,' Aniko?"

"Yes, Papa-san," the little girl replied.

"Here is one." She pointed to a large carton nearby.

Mr. Kito walked over to the box. "This is strange," he remarked. "It is addressed to The Kito Shop, Barham. But it must be for me."

He pried open the top. "Yes," he said, "the lanterns are here." He took out a few. They had been collapsed for easier packing. At each end of the lantern was a circle of thin wood painted black. In between the wooden circles was fluted paper. They were in various colors.

"How pretty!" Honey Bunch exclaimed.

Mr. Kito examined the lanterns. "These don't look exactly like the ones I ordered," he mused.

Just then Nikkio spoke up from the other side of the room. "Papa san, here is another box marked 'lanterns.'"

His father went to look at the packing case. This one was addressed to The Tokyo Shop, Barham.

"These are the lanterns I ordered," Mr. Kito observed, as he lifted one from the box. "I'll put several in the window. They will make people look at the store tonight!"

"What will you do with the other lanterns, Papa-san?" Aniko asked.

19

The Japanese man looked thoughtful, then said, "I think someone at the lantern factory in Japan made a mistake and sent me two orders of lanterns. I will keep the extra shipment and pay for it when I receive a bill."

"The lanterns are so pretty," Honey Bunch observed. "Lots of people will want to buy them."

"I hope so," Mr. Kito remarked. "Now I will trim the window. Are you tired of unpacking?"

"Oh no!" Norman exclaimed. "There are lots of packages to unwrap. And we haven't found the paper birds yet!"

Mr. Kito smiled and left the room with an armful of lanterns.

"Let's open this box next," Honey Bunch suggested, going over to a large one with the address painted on in thick strokes of black ink.

The carton was wrapped in shiny brown paper and securely tied with heavy twine. Norman and Nikkio took turns trying to untie the cord. Neither of them was able to do it.

"I'll get some scissors," Aniko volunteered. She ran to the front of the shop and soon returned with a pair. "Papa-san says we must be very careful and not cut ourselves," she reported with a little smile.

Norman took the scissors and soon had cut the twine in several places. Nikkio tore off the paper and lifted the lid of the carton.

Honey Bunch peered in. "More tea cups!" she announced. "Remember Norman, just five of a kind!"

The children set to work unwrapping the delicate cups. This time Honey Bunch took them from the box while the others arranged them on the table.

Suddenly Honey Bunch exclaimed, "What's this, Aniko? What are these funny marks?" She held up a sheet of very thin, crisp paper. It was covered with spidery-looking black drawings.

"That is Japanese writing," Aniko explained. "Let me see it." The little girl took the sheet of paper and examined it carefully.

"It is a letter," she said, "and I think I can read it. Mama-san is teaching both Nikkio and me to read Japanese."

Slowly Aniko translated into English:

"I am a little girl. I am eight years old. My name is Honey Blossom. Papa-san is looking for our cousin, Henry Yakura, in your country. He has a big secret to tell Cousin Henry. Will whoever gets this box please help us find Cousin Henry."

Honey Bunch and Norman and the Japanese children looked at one another in astonishment. "I wish we could help Honey Blossom!" Honey Bunch said. "Maybe we *can* find her cousin Henry."

"How?" Norman asked. "The United States is a mighty big place!"

Honey Bunch agreed and for a moment looked sad. Then she brightened. "Maybe we can find some clues. Will you help us, Aniko and Nick?"

The Japanese children nodded eagerly and the cowlick in Nikkio's black hair bobbed in excitement.

"We are very happy to assist you," Aniko said, "but tomorrow we must help our Mama-san. We are going to move into our honorable house."

"Pollywogs!" Norman exclaimed. "I wish I could move. It must be fun!"

"Do you want to move away so we can't play together any more?" Honey Bunch teased him.

Norman looked embarrassed. "N-no," he stammered. "I guess I don't really want to move!"

"We're going to live in a house on Grove Street," Aniko announced proudly.

"Grove Street!" Honey Bunch exclaimed. "Why, that's where I live!"

Mr. Kito had come into the room during the conversation about moving. "Perhaps we will be neighbors. That will be nice for Aniko and Nikkio," he said.

Norman snapped his fingers. "Say!" he exclaimed. "Maybe you're the ones that queer man was looking for!"

"Queer man? Looking for me?" Mr. Kito repeated.

"Yes," Honey Bunch said. "He asked Norman and me if we knew a Japanese family."

"What did the man look like?" Mr. Kito asked curiously.

"He was thin and had blond hair," Honey Bunch replied.

"And he blinked his eyes all the time!" Norman added.

Mr. Kito shook his head. "I don't know anyone like that. I wonder why he would be looking for us?"

CHAPTER III

MOVING DAY

HONEY BUNCH and Norman looked puzzled when Mr. Kito said he did not know the man who had been asking for a Japanese family.

"If he comes back, we'll tell him you're moving in tomorrow," Norman said cheerfully.

When Mr. Kito gave the address of his home, Honey Bunch said, "That's near where Ida Camp lives! She's one of our playmates!"

"And your house is only about two blocks from Honey Bunch and me!" Norman exclaimed. "We'll have fun playing together."

"Where have you been staying?" Honey Bunch asked the Japanese children.

"At the Sunset Motel," Aniko explained. "We've been there while Papa-san has been getting his store ready to open."

"Before that we lived in San Francisco," Nikkio spoke up.

"And before that we were in Tokyo, Japan!" his sister chimed in.

24

Mr. Kito explained that the family had planned to move into the Grove Street house several days earlier but had been delayed by the painters.

Aniko had been examining the rest of the packing boxes. Now she picked up one which seemed very light. "Maybe the flying birds are in this package, Papa-san," she said.

Sure enough, when the box was opened there were the little black-and-white birds as well as other small Japanese toys.

Mr. Kito took out one of the birds and gave it to Honey Bunch. "I make you a *presento* of this," he said. "You have helped us a great deal today. And for you, little Norman, here is a Japanese puzzle toy."

Honey Bunch and Norman were delighted with their gifts and thanked Mr. Kito for his kindness.

"Papa-san," Nikkio said, "Honey Bunch found this note." He picked up the paper with the Japanese writing on it.

His father took the note and read it. Then, handing it back, he remarked, "This is very odd. Perhaps the little girl is playing a game. Henry Yakura is a common name in Japan."

"I'm going to try to find him for Honey

25

Blossom," Honey Bunch announced. "I have to help people with a name like mine."

Mr. Kito laughed. "That is a good idea."

At this moment Mrs. Miller returned from her shopping trip. "Come, children," she called, "it's time to go home."

Norman offered to carry the bowl with the Japanese goldfish while Honey Bunch took the paper bird and Norman's puzzle toy. They said good-by to Aniko and Nikkio and promised to see them the next day.

When Honey Bunch and Norman reached the Mortons' house they said good-by. Norman waved and scrambled over the fence. "See you later, alligator!" he called.

"I'm going to call Ida Camp and some of my other friends and tell them about Aniko and Nikkio," Honey Bunch told Mrs. Miller.

By the time she had finished her telephoning, Honey Bunch had talked to Cora and Kitty Williams and Grace Winters as well as Ida Camp. She also called little Elmer Gray to let him know what was done about the trade gift. Then she mentioned the Japanese children to him.

"I want to play with them, too," said Elmer.

Honey Bunch had just left the telephone

26

when her mother returned home from a garden club meeting. Edith Morton was a slim, pretty woman with a warm smile.

"Mother," Honey Bunch cried as she ran to kiss her, "I've had the most scrumptious time today!" She told about the visit to The Tokyo Shop and meeting the Kitos. "And they're moving into a house right here on Grove Street tomorrow morning!" she concluded breathlessly.

"I'll look forward to meeting your new friends, dear," Mrs. Morton said.

That evening Honey Bunch sat at the supper table with her mother and her tall, athletic-looking father. Suddenly she remembered the strange man who had questioned her and Norman that afternoon.

"He asked us if we knew a Japanese family around here," the little girl said. "We told him we didn't. Then when we met Aniko and Nick they said they were going to move here! Isn't that funny?"

"Quite a coincidence," Mr. Morton agreed. "Evidently the man had found out that Mr. Kito was going to live on Grove Street and thought he'd already moved here."

"Mr. Kito said they couldn't move in earlier

27

because the painters were still working," Honey Bunch explained. "I guess the man with the blinking eyes didn't know that."

Right after breakfast the next morning Norman came tumbling over the fence and shouted, "Honey Bunch! Honey Bunch! Quick!"

Mrs. Miller came hurrying to the kitchen door. "Mercy, Norman!" she said. "What's the matter?"

"I want Honey Bunch to go down and watch Aniko and Nick move into their house!"

Mrs. Miller gave a great sigh. "You made such a fuss, I thought the house must be on fire!"

Norman grinned. "I'm sorry, Mrs. Miller. Is Honey Bunch ready?"

"She's eating her waffles. I don't suppose you'd want any?" the woman asked with a twinkle in her eye.

"Pollywogs!" Norman cried. "You know I love waffles!"

"Come on in." Mrs. Miller pushed open the screen door. "I have two hot ones for you!"

Honey Bunch was alone at the breakfast table when Norman joined her. Mrs. Miller put the golden-brown waffles in front of him and he carefully filled each little hollow square with butter and syrup.

"Yumm!" Norman squinted his eyes as he took the first bite. "These are great!"

He ate the two crisp cakes, then he and Honey Bunch started off down the street. When they reached the Kitos' house, the two little Williams girls and Elmer Gray were already there. In a few minutes Ida Camp and Grace Winters walked up.

"I've never seen a little Japanese boy or girl," Elmer said.

"You'll love them!" Honey Bunch observed. "They are cute-looking and very polite!"

At that moment a car drove up and Mr. and Mrs. Kito, with the two children, got out. Honey Bunch introduced her little friends to the Japanese.

Mrs. Kito was small and pretty. She wore her black hair in a bun at the back of her neck. Her dark eyes twinkled as she said good morning to the children.

"We just had word that the truck from California is here in Barham," Mr. Kito told them. "Have you come to see us move into our new home?"

Honey Bunch nodded. "We thought we could help you carry things in. We're all glad you're going to live here."

Mrs. Kito bowed politely. "Thank you very much," she said. "We are happy that Aniko and Nikkio will have children to play with."

Norman had been peering up the street. Now he jumped up and down and cried, "Here comes the truck!"

In another minute the huge moving van pulled into the driveway. Two men jumped down from the cab. "Mr. Taki Kito?" one of them asked.

Mr. Kito bowed in reply. "We are ready."

The men let down the tailgate of the truck and began to unload the contents. First came a tricycle, then a wooden rocking horse, then a box of toys. Each of the children picked up a small article and carried it into the house.

There were several long, low tables and a few chairs which the moving men took in. Then they returned for another load.

Honey Bunch had been watching them. Now she whispered to Norman, "I don't see any beds. Where do you s'pose they are?"

Aniko who had been standing near Honey Bunch overheard the question. "We Japanese don't use beds like yours. We sleep on *futons* spread on the floor."

"What are futons?" Ida Camp asked.

Aniko explained that they are padded quilts.

30

"We keep them in a cupboard during the day-
time and bring them out when we are ready to
sleep."

Nikko pointed to many rolls of quilts piled
in one corner of the truck. "There are the
futons," he said.

"We also use a small pillow which Americans
think is very hard," Aniko added, smiling.

"Let's each carry in a futon," Grace Winters
suggested.

All the children thought this would be fun

and each one picked up a roll. Elmer, who was too little to handle one alone, ran ahead to hold the front door open.

What a parade it was! Eight children, each with a rolled quilt over his shoulder, trooped into the house. Mr. and Mrs. Kito laughed when they saw the procession.

As the children passed Elmer Gray, he backed up so they could get by. As he did he bumped into a huge vase which one of the moving men had just set down on a low table.

Honey Bunch saw the vase topple. At once she dropped her futon and dashed over. She was just in time! The beautiful vase was about to crash on the floor when Honey Bunch grabbed it.

"Oh, thank you," Mrs. Kito cried. "I would not like to have anything happen to my dragon vase. It is very old and has been in my family for many years!"

"Where is the dragon?" asked Elmer.

Mrs. Kito showed him how the figure of a dragon had been worked into the design painted on the vase. This gave Norman an idea. He had noticed that one of the futons had come unrolled. Now he pulled it up over his head. With his tongue out and darting from side to side, Norman began to prance about the room.

"Grrr! Look at me!" he shouted. "I'm a dragon!"

Honey Bunch giggled. "I don't think dragons growl," she said. "You sound like a bear!"

"I'm a dragon and I say *grrr!*" Norman insisted.

All the children laughed and started to chase Norman, pretending to capture him. They played this game until they were out of breath. Then Mrs. Kito brought out a box of Japanese cookies and passed them around.

Honey Bunch noticed an open carton which was full of bright-colored objects. "What are those, Aniko?" she asked.

The little Japanese girl jumped up and went over to the packing box. "These are my parasols," she explained. "I collect them."

She took one out and opened it. The parasol was made of pale blue paper with a delicate design of pink cherry blossoms. Aniko put the parasol over her shoulder and twirled it as she walked.

Honey Bunch and the other girls clapped. Then Aniko gave each girl a parasol and showed her how to spin the colorful umbrellas. Some of the parasols were decorated with flower designs. Others had pictures of tall, thin Japanese dancers in bright-colored kimonos.

Norman was a little jealous because he hadn't received a parasol. "Do boys in Japan carry parasols?" he asked Nikkio.

The Japanese boy shook his head. Then he grinned and said, "But they go fishing with them sometimes."

"Fishing!" Norman cried in amazement. "How could you go fishing with a parasol?"

Mr. Kito had heard the discussion. Now he explained. "In one of the bays off Japan, the fishermen use what they call an 'umbrella boat.' "

"Is it made out of an umbrella?" Norman asked, puzzled.

"No." Mr. Kito chuckled. "The fisherman fastens a big parasol onto an upright pole in his boat. Then he turns it so it will keep off the rain or sun. And the umbrella also acts as a sail."

Norman's eyes shone. "That sounds keen!" he exclaimed. "It would be fun to do that on the pond in Barham Park!"

The other children had gone outdoors again. Quickly Norman ran after them.

The moving men had dropped two heavy

mats on the ground beside the truck. Norman turned a somersault on one of them. Nikkio clapped his hands. "You are a tumbler! Aniko and I too can tumble!"

He beckoned his sister who ran onto the mat. Nikkio dropped to his knees and Aniko quickly climbed to her brother's shoulders. Then with a sudden motion he tossed her off. She turned a somersault in the air and landed on her feet. Even the moving men clapped.

"Whee!"

"You're good!"

"Show us how!" the other children exclaimed.

"Let's show them our stunt, Honey Bunch!" Norman proposed.

His little playmate agreed. In a flash Honey Bunch and Norman stood on their hands. Then as Ida Camp hummed a slow tune, they did a little dance.

"Very good!" Nikkio applauded. "I have never seen an upside-down dance before."

By this time the moving men had finished their work. They came out of the house and began to put the mats back into the big van.

Aniko said to her new friends, "If you want to come inside the house, I will show you how we arrange our furniture."

35

The children followed her into the living room where she pointed out a small alcove in one corner. "This will be the most important place in our house," Aniko explained. "It is called the *tokonoma*. Mama-san will put our best scroll here and her nicest flower arrangements. When we want to be quiet and think, we sit down and look at the tokonoma."

Honey Bunch turned to see if Norman had heard this, but he was not in the group.

"Where's Norman?" she asked Nikkio.

The little Japanese boy said he did not know. Calling her playmate's name, Honey Bunch ran through the house. The other children went outside and searched the yard.

Norman was not in sight. Where had he gone?

CHAPTER IV

AN UMBRELLA BOAT

"Who saw Norman last?" Honey Bunch asked.

"I did," Elmer Gray spoke up.

"Where was he?"

"He was helping roll up those big mats and put them into the truck," the four-year-old replied.

"I'm sure he wasn't in the house when Aniko was showing us the tokonoma," Grace Winters put in. "Maybe he went home."

Mr. and Mrs. Kito joined the children outside and were disturbed to learn of Norman's disappearance. They let Honey Bunch phone the Clark house but Norman was not there. She returned to the others and said worriedly, "Do you suppose he got wrapped up in a mat by mistake?"

"And was carried away on the truck!" Elmer said, his blue eyes widening.

Honey Bunch started running down the street. "You can't catch the truck!" Aniko called after her. "It has been gone a long time!"

"I'll get Mr. Reilly!" Honey Bunch shouted back. "He'll know how to find Norman."

It was not her puppy Honey Bunch meant, but Officer Reilly who was usually directing traffic on the corner near the Mortons' home. He was a good friend of Honey Bunch's and often helped her when she was trying to solve a mystery.

Now she saw him. He had just held up a line of cars to let an old woman walk across the street. When Officer Reilly caught sight of Honey Bunch, he waved the cars on. Then he came over to the sidewalk to talk to her.

"Good morning, Honey Bunch," he called. "How's my girl?"

"I'm just fine, Mr. Reilly," she replied, "but Norman's lost!" Her blue eyes filled with tears.

"Lost, you say? Now, you just tell me all about it and I'm sure we can find him in no time!"

Honey Bunch told about the moving van which had brought the Kitos' furniture and how Norman had been seen putting the mats back in the truck.

"I'm afraid he's been rolled up and taken away in the van!" she ended with a little sob.

"Well, we'll get him back," Mr. Reilly said kindly. "I'll find out the name of the moving company and have the truck picked up."

"I know. It's Wooley!" Honey Bunch exclaimed. "I read it."

"Good girl," said Mr. Reilly.

He turned to a metal box on a pole and unlocked it. Inside was a telephone to call police headquarters.

The policeman asked for a squad car for the search. When it arrived, the driver took over Mr. Reilly's station, so he could go with Honey Bunch to locate the truck. Aniko and Nikkio had run up with their father and were invited to go.

"I am sure the truck was going west from here," Mr. Kito informed the policeman.

"Headquarters has phoned ahead to the next town to have the truck stopped," Mr. Reilly said. "We should be able to catch up with it."

The police car sped through Barham and out onto the westbound highway. Nikkio squirmed with excitement. Honey Bunch and Aniko stared tensely ahead.

Suddenly Nikkio shouted, "There's a truck by the side of the road up there."

When they reached the truck they found a State Trooper on a motorcycle talking to the driver.

"Is this the van you want, Reilly?" the trooper called out as the police car stopped.

"That's it," Officer Reilly replied cheerfully. "We think maybe they have a boy with them by mistake."

The van driver looked amazed. "I'm sure none of those kids got in the truck but you're welcome to look!"

His helper climbed down and opened the big rear doors of the van. Officer Reilly and the State Trooper jumped up into the truck and carefully searched among the rolled-up mats. Norman was not there!

"I'm glad of that," said Honey Bunch, and started to think where else they might find Norman.

Officer Reilly thanked the trooper and told the truck driver he was sorry for the delay. Then he returned to the police car.

"You know, Mr. Reilly," Honey Bunch said seriously, "I think Norman is at the pond in Barham Park!"

"Barham Park!" the officer exclaimed. "Now why would you think that?"

"You'll see!" she replied mysteriously.

"All aboard for Barham Park then!" Officer Reilly said jovially.

A short while later they drove into the pretty park and turned onto the road which led past the pond.

As they neared the shallow body of water Aniko called out, "There's something out in the middle!"

"It's Norman!" Honey Bunch cried.

Sure enough, there was the little boy, standing on a small raft. He was holding an open parasol! As they watched, a little gust of wind came up. It caught the parasol and sped the raft toward the shore.

Thud! The small raft hit the bank! Norman flew through the air and landed on the muddy shore.

Officer Reilly and Honey Bunch jumped out of the car, Nikkio and Aniko followed. They ran toward Norman who was just picking himself up.

When he saw them, he turned red. "I—I was trying out Aniko's parasol as an umbrella boat," he explained sheepishly.

Norman went over to catch the parasol which was about to blow away. He looked at it carefully, then handed the paper umbrella to Aniko.

"I don't think it's hurt," he told her. "I really hope it isn't." Aniko assured him the parasol was all right.

Officer Reilly took all the children home and Honey Bunch thanked him for his help. Later that afternoon she was seated on the porch with her mother.

"What are you thinking about," Mrs. Morton asked. "You look very solemn. Is something the matter?"

"I'm worried about Honey Blossom in Japan," Honey Bunch replied. "I want to find her Cousin Henry but I don't know how to do it."

"Why don't you write to her and find out more about Henry?" Mrs. Morton suggested.

"Oh Mother! That's a scrumptious idea!" Honey Bunch cried. "And Aniko can put the letter into Japanese for me!"

Honey Bunch ran into the house and in a minute returned with a pad of paper and a pencil. Then after much thought and her mother's help in spelling words, she wrote:

Dear Honey Blossom: I got your letter and will try to find your cousin Henry. What is the secret your father wants to tell him?

Honey Bunch Morton

She showed the note to her mother. "Is it all right?" she asked.

Mrs. Morton said she thought the letter was fine. Then she suggested, "How would you like to have a little garden party for Aniko and

Nikkio to welcome them to the neighborhood? You could ask them now."

"Oh Mother, that would be wonderful!" Honey Bunch cried.

It was decided that the party would be two days later. All the children would be asked to come in Japanese costume as in honor of Aniko and Nikkio.

Honey Bunch hurried off to the Kitos' house with the invitation and her letter. When she met Aniko she asked, "Will you please put my letter to Honey Blossom in Japanese?"

Aniko read the letter. Then she got a piece of paper and a special brush and ink. She carefully drew the characters in Japanese.

"That looks beautiful!" Honey Bunch exclaimed admiringly. "And I brought an overseas air-mail stamp so the letter will get to Tokyo real fast!"

When Honey Bunch told Mrs. Kito about the children's party, the Japanese woman said she would make some Japanese cookies for Aniko and Nikkio to bring. Mr. Kito came home just then. When he heard about the party, he said:

"If it's to be Japanese, you should have some Japanese lanterns."

"Oh yes, Papa-san." Aniko agreed.

"I'll send over that extra carton of lanterns and you can string them around the yard," the shop owner offered.

Honey Bunch thanked Mr. and Mrs. Kito for their help and hurried home to tell her mother. All the children said they would be glad to come to the party and Mrs. Miller promised to make some strawberry ice cream.

When the party day arrived Mrs. Morton and Mrs. Miller strung the Japanese lanterns on a clothesline between the apple tree and the lowest branch of the big oak. Honey Bunch put on a pretty kimono and sandals. Then she set the picnic table with a gay paper tablecloth. At each place she laid a paper napkin in the shape of a Japanese parasol.

"Doesn't it look scrumptious?" she asked her mother.

"Yes, it does, dear."

At this moment Norman climbed over the fence. He had on navy-blue shorts and a blue jacket with wide sleeves. His black hair was plastered down with water.

"Norman, you look very Japanese," Honey Bunch exclaimed.

Her playmate seemed pleased. "Nick lent me this coat," he explained. "It's a happy coat, and this means I'm a fireman." He turned to show her a round design in the middle of the back.

Just then Cora and Kitty Williams, Grace Winters, Ida Camp, and little Elmer Gray came into the yard. They all wore bright-colored Japanese kimonos except Elmer. He had on shorts and a T-shirt and a big straw coolie hat on his head. A long braid of black hair was fastened to the hat and hung down his back.

"My daddy said the braid was Chinese," Elmer explained, "but I saw it in the costume store and I like it." He smiled impishly.

"Here come Aniko and Nick," Norman cried.

He ran up to take the box of cookies from the little Japanese girl. But Mrs. Miller appeared at this moment and took the package from Norman's arms. He looked annoyed.

"Remember, Norman," Honey Bunch called, "you have on a happy coat!"

"What a nice surprise," said Aniko. "You are all Japanese today."

Nikkio smiled and bowed to his new playmates. Then he said, "Happy is spelled *h-a-p-p-i* and means a coat worn by Japanese workmen."

46

"I'm happy anyway!" Norman shouted, turning a somersault. "Let's play some games."

"Musical chairs first," Ida proposed.

Everyone agreed. The chairs from the picnic table were placed in a line and Mrs. Morton put a record on the phonograph Honey Bunch brought out. When the music stopped suddenly, there was a great rush for the chairs.

"Elmer's out!" Ida Camp called. The little boy was having so much trouble keeping his big hat on that he had missed a chair!

Ida Camp tripped on her kimono and was the next one out. The game went on until there was only one chair and the two Japanese children left. Aniko and Nikkio circled it slowly.

The music stopped. Nikkio plopped into the seat. Aniko landed on his lap! Everyone laughed.

"Here is your prize," Honey Bunch said, and handed the pleased winner a big red-and-blue ball.

"Now we'll have a peanut race," Honey Bunch announced. She placed two small bowls on the grass at each side of the yard. The bowl at one end was filled with unshelled peanuts.

"Elmer wants to referee," Norman informed her.

He and Honey Bunch chose sides. Norman

47

took Nikkio, Cora Williams, and Grace Winters. Honey Bunch's team consisted of Kitty Williams, Ida Camp, and Aniko.

At a signal from Elmer, Nikkio took one of the peanuts in the bowl on a teaspoon, ran across the yard, and dropped the nut in the empty dish. Kitty Williams did the same. The race went on until Aniko scooped up the last peanut from her team's bowl. Carefully she ran across the grass and dropped it in the other bowl!

"The winner is Honey Bunch's team!" Elmer announced.

"Good, Aniko!" Honey Bunch cried. "Our side won!"

They all praised Aniko for learning the game so quickly and Honey Bunch gave her a little American baby-doll for a prize.

"Refreshments now!" Mrs. Morton called.

When the children had taken their places at the table Mrs. Miller brought out big dishes of luscious homemade strawberry ice cream. Then she put two plates with the pretty Japanese cookies on the table.

"I love ice cream!" Aniko said, her dark eyes sparkling. Nikkio bobbed his head in agreement.

The last cookie had just disappeared from the

plates and the last bite of ice cream had just been eaten, when a man walked into the yard. He was short and stocky with black hair.

"My name is Kitts," he explained. "I live at 64 Oak Street." He spoke very rapidly.

"What is it you want, Mr. Kitts?" Mrs Morton asked pleasantly.

"I want my paper lanterns," the man replied gruffly.

"Yours?" Honey Bunch said in surprise. "Mr. Kito loaned these to us. They belong to him."

"Oh, no, they don't," the stranger persisted. He pulled a note from his pocket. "Read this if you don't believe me. It's from Mr. Kito."

Mrs. Morton read the note in which Mr. Kito said that the lanterns appeared to have been shipped to him by mistake and were intended for Mr. Kitts. The similarity of the names had evidently caused the mix-up.

Honey Bunch looked doubtful. "I'm going to phone Mr. Kito," she whispered to Norman.

In a minute she was back. "Mr. Kito says the lanterns do belong to Mr. Kitts," she reported sadly. "I guess we'll have to take them down."

"I'll do it," Norman volunteered.

While the little girls helped Mrs. Morton and

49

Mrs. Miller clear the table, the stocky man paced restlessly up and down the driveway. Norman climbed the apple tree and untied the clothesline.

The row of lanterns dropped to the grass as Norman let himself down from the apple tree. *Crunch!* In his haste he stepped on one of the lanterns!

"Pollywogs! he exclaimed in horror. "I've smashed it!"

CHAPTER V

A STICKY CAT

WHEN Norman saw that he had broken one of the paper lanterns, he looked around at the other children. Most of them were busy and had not noticed the accident.

But little Elmer Gray had seen what had happened. "You spoiled that lantern," Elmer said accusingly.

"Sshh!" Norman put his finger to his lips warningly. "Look, Elmer, you and I are friends, aren't we?" he asked.

Elmer nodded vigorously.

"Well then, promise me you won't tell yet what happened to the lantern," Norman urged. "I'm going to try to fix it."

"I won't tell," Elmer agreed.

"I'll hide it till later."

Norman picked up the smashed lantern and carried it into the Mortons' garage. He put it behind an old tire, then ran back to the yard.

Honey Bunch and Mrs. Miller were packing the other lanterns in the carton.

"Where have you been Norman?" Honey Bunch asked.

"Nowhere, special," her playmate replied, trying to look unconcerned.

"You act sort of funny," Honey Bunch observed. "What have you been doing?"

"Nothing," Norman said and quickly turned to pick up some of the lanterns.

"Leave him alone, Honey Bunch," Mrs. Miller advised. Then she added something in a whisper.

Mr. Kitts left with his box of paper lanterns and the children came up to say thank you for the party and bid good-by to Honey Bunch.

Norman, however, hung back and kept very quiet.

Ida Camp noticed this. "What's the matter, Norman. Don't you feel well?" she asked.

"Don't bother Norman," Honey Bunch spoke up. "He won't talk because he has a lot of gold."

Norman looked puzzled. "Gold? What do you mean, Honey Bunch?" But the little girl had walked off with Ida and did not reply.

The next morning Mrs. Kito telephoned.

She invited Honey Bunch to come play with Aniko. "Nikkio is going to The Tokyo Shop to help his father," she added.

Mrs. Morton gave her permission and Honey Bunch hurried off to the Kito home. She found Ida Camp and Grace Winters there.

"Would you like to play Battledore and Shuttlecock?" Aniko asked her three guests as she led them into the back yard.

"How do you play it?" Honey Bunch asked.

Aniko explained that there were two players on a side and they batted a shuttlecock back and forth across a net with a battledore.

"That sounds like our game of badminton," Grace remarked.

When Aniko brought out the equipment, Ida exclaimed, "It *is* badminton, but look at the rackets!"

They were very different from the ones the girls were accustomed to using. Instead of being plain wood, these were decorated with figures of men and women.

One racket was painted with the picture of a Japanese woman in a colorful kimono. Fancy ornaments had been stuck in her hair.

"Look at this one!" Honey Bunch exclaimed. She held up a racket on which was the head of a man. His black hair was gathered up into a topknot and he had a very fierce expression on his face.

"These are all pictures of famous actors and actresses," Aniko explained. "But I do not remember their names."

Sides were drawn by lot and it was decided that Honey Bunch and Aniko would play against the other two girls.

Ida and Grace won the first game. Honey Bunch and Aniko did better in the second game. Honey Bunch was just running to hit the shuttlecock when a man walked into the yard.

"It's Mr. Kitts!" Aniko exclaimed, throwing down her racket. "I'll see what he wants."

When she reached the caller, she bowed and said, "May I help you, Mr. Kitts?"

"You can give me that other lantern!" he demanded angrily.

Honey Bunch ran up to stand beside her little friend. "What other lantern?" she asked. "You took all the lanterns from my house yesterday!"

"No I didn't, and you know it!" Mr. Kitts shouted, shaking his fist.

"We don't know anything about another lantern," Aniko said firmly. "Maybe if you go

54

to my father's store he could find the missing one for you."

The man merely grunted. He muttered something under his breath and left the yard.

"I have to go home," Honey Bunch announced suddenly to her friends.

"Why?" Ida Camp asked, surprised. "We haven't finished our game!"

"I'm sorry. Maybe I can play some more this afternoon," Honey Bunch replied. "But I just thought of something important I have to do at home."

She left her friends with puzzled looks on their faces. Honey Bunch ran out of the Kitos' yard and down Grove Street toward her own home.

"Norman acted very funny yesterday," the little girl told herself. "Maybe he knows something about the missing paper lantern."

Honey Bunch ran into her yard and toward the fence separating it from the Clarks' yard. Just as she was about to call Norman, she heard familiar voices coming from the other side of the fence.

"Did you tell anybody," one voice asked.

"That's Norman," Honey Bunch thought.

Then she heard little Elmer Gray speak.

"No, I told you I wouldn't, didn't I?"

"Good boy!" Norman praised him.

"Where did you get all the gold, Norman?" Elmer asked. "Will you show it to me?"

"I don't know what you're talking about. I don't have any gold," Norman replied in a puzzled tone.

"Honey Bunch says you have lots of gold," Elmer persisted.

"Pooh!" Norman said airily. "She was only fooling. Let's go see if that—uh—thing is still there."

He stood up and Honey Bunch had just time enough to duck behind some bushes before Norman climbed over the fence and pulled Elmer after him.

"Come on!" Norman looked around carefully, then he and Elmer walked into the Mortons' garage.

Honey Bunch crept to the door and looked inside. Norman was just lifting the broken paper lantern from behind the tire.

"What is that?" Honey Bunch called.

Norman jumped up like a jack-in-the-box. "Why—why," he stammered. "It's—it's just one of the paper lanterns."

"What are you doing with it?" Honey Bunch asked accusingly.

Norman, shamefaced, admitted that he had broken and hidden the lantern. "I came back to try to fix it," said the little boy. "I didn't think that Mr. Kitts would miss one old lantern."

Honey Bunch told Norman that Mr. Kitts had come to the Kitos' home in search of the missing lantern. He had been very angry not to find it.

"Pollywogs!" Norman looked worriedly at the torn paper and broken wood in his hand. "Maybe I can't fix this good enough."

"I'll help you," Honey Bunch offered. Then she added, "Let's tell Aniko and Nikkio what happened. I'm sure they'll know what to do. Aniko told me her mother taught them to make things out of paper."

"I'll go get them!" Norman cried and dashed out of the yard followed by Elmer Gray.

Honey Bunch carried the broken lantern to the picnic table and surveyed the wreckage. The paper was ripped in several places and the round black wood collar at the top was broken.

The little girl left the lantern and went into the kitchen where Mrs. Miller was shelling peas. "Please, may I have some glue and some of that sticky tape." Honey Bunch asked the woman.

"It's all there in the table drawer," Mrs. Miller replied. "Why do you want it?"

"One of the Japanese paper lanterns is broken," Honey Bunch explained. "Norman's bringing Aniko and Nick and we're all going to mend it."

Mrs. Miller did not ask how the lantern had been broken. Honey Bunch was glad, for she did not want to have to tell on Norman.

"Well, don't let Norman get glue all over everything," Mrs. Miller advised.

By the time Honey Bunch had collected the mending materials Norman was back with Aniko and Nikkio. He explained that Ida, Grace, and Elmer had had to go home.

"I just got home myself," Nikkio said. "That Mr. Kitts came to the shop and he was shouting that he had to have the other lantern and would not take any of ours!"

"I'm glad you found this one, Honey Bunch," Aniko said. "Norman told us what happened to the lantern. I'm sure we can fix it."

The four children sat down on the chairs at the picnic table to work. Aniko lifted the battered lantern and examined it. The top piece hung to the paper by only one small shred.

"I think we can take this off and repair it separately," the little Japanese girl said.

The round wooden collar was broken in several places. While Nikkio held the splintered

58

pieces, Aniko spread glue on each end. Then he pressed them together firmly.

"There!" She laid the collar down on the table. "We'll let it dry. I think it will hold."

"Shall we mend the paper next?" Honey Bunch asked.

When Aniko nodded Honey Bunch picked up the roll of stick tape and tore off a small piece. She carefully fastened two pieces of the torn paper together with the tape.

"See!" Honey Bunch held up the lantern. "I don't think the tears are going to show very much!"

"Let me fix a place!" Norman cried impatiently. He picked up the roll of sticky tape and began to pull off a long piece. As he did this, Lady Clare jumped to the table and rubbed against the little boy.

"Get away, Lady Clare," Norman said, "You'll get stuck."

But his warning came too late. The long ribbon of sticky tape caught on the cat's fur. Startled, Lady Clare leaped down from the table, pulling the roll with her.

Round and round she flew, trying to get free. But the more she twisted, the more entangled she became!

Norman and Nikkio were doubled up with

laughter as Honey Bunch and Aniko tried to catch Lady Clare. Finally Honey Bunch grabbed her pet up in her arms and quieted her.

"Poor sticky kitty," she said.

"You mean she's a stuck-up cat," Norman chortled.

Aniko gently pulled off the tape. It was ruined for use, so Honey Bunch went to get another. The repair work continued, with the children taking turns. Soon the lantern looked whole again.

"I think this wood is strong enough now," Aniko said. "I'll fasten it to the paper with some more of the tape."

She did this very carefully. "Now let's see if the lantern will fold up as it's supposed to do."

Aniko passed the lantern to Honey Bunch

who put one hand on the top and the other under the base. As she pushed the two ends together she heard a slight rattle.

"What was that?" she asked, startled.

"There's something in the bottom!" Norman exclaimed.

"Should there be anything inside?" Honey Bunch asked Aniko.

The little Japanese girl shook her head. She took the lantern and juggled it. Sure enough, this time the rattle was quite distinct.

"It must be a false bottom!" Honey Bunch cried.

"Open it up!" Norman urged.

Carefully, Honey Bunch pulled the paper away from the round black base. Then she pressed hard on the side of the thin wood until it gave way.

"Oh!" she cried as a string of gleaming pearls fell out.

CHAPTER VI

THE JEWELER'S SURPRISE

"BEADS!" Norman exclaimed. He quickly grabbed the string of pearls and draped it over his head. "See, I'm a king!" he cried, marching around the yard. "This is my crown!"

The other children laughed. Then Honey Bunch looked serious. "I wonder if Mr. Kitts knew the pearls were in the lantern," she mused. "That might be why he was so eager to get it back."

"It is possible," Nikkio agreed. "The lanterns are not expensive, and Papa-san wondered why Mr. Kitts was so upset about losing one."

"Maybe these are real pearls, not just beads!" Honey Bunch exclaimed suddenly.

"Many pearls come from Japan," Aniko spoke up. "But why would Mr. Kitts have them sent in a paper lantern?"

"I don't know, but let's find out if they're really pearls or just plain beads," Honey Bunch suggested.

"How can you tell?" Norman wondered.

"We can take them down to the Barham Jewelry Company and ask Mr. Peters," his playmate replied. Mr. Peters was a friend of Mr. Morton's and the owner of the town's best jewelry store.

Mrs. Morton was busy sewing upstairs when Honey Bunch called in to her, "We're all going down the street. All right?"

"Yes," her mother replied, "but don't stay too long."

Honey Bunch and Norman and the two Japanese children hurried to the jewelry store.

"Hello there!" Mr. Peters called jovially as they entered his shop.

Honey Bunch introduced Aniko and Nikkio. Then she laid the string of beads on the counter. "Please, Mr. Peters," she asked, "can you tell us whether these are real pearls or only make-believe ones?"

"I think I can," the man replied. He put a small magnifying glass to his eye and bent over the beads. Slowly he ran them through his fingers. Then he took them to the door to examine them by daylight.

He returned with a smile. "I'd say you have an extra fine string of cultured pearls here," he said.

"You mean they're real?" Honey Bunch cried out.

"Yes."

The children were amazed. "Why are the pearls cultured?" Norman asked.

Mr. Peters explained that real pearls are formed when a tiny foreign substance accidentally becomes lodged under an oyster's shell. Many layers of nacre—mother-of-pearl—grow around it and build a pearl.

"But why is it cultured?" Norman persisted.

"Perfect pearls formed this way are extremely rare," the jeweler went on. "Some years ago a Japanese man started making pearls artificially. He invented a process whereby a speck of shell was inserted into the flesh of oys-

ters. These oysters are kept in underwater bins, called beds, and carefully watched. The speck irritates the oyster and he keeps covering it with fluids which make it into a cultured pearl."

"Does it take a long time to make a pearl?" Honey Bunch asked with interest.

"Indeed it does—about seven years," Mr. Peters replied.

Aniko nodded vigorously. "That is right," she said. "Papa-san has a friend in Japan who owns a pearl farm."

Norman grinned. "If I had a farm I'd rather grow pigs than pearls!"

The jeweler smiled. "This string of pearls is worth many hundreds of dollars. Do they belong to your mother, Honey Bunch?"

"No," the little girl replied. "We found them in a paper lantern."

"You found them!" Mr. Peters exclaimed in amazement. "Where was this lantern?"

Honey Bunch and Norman told the jeweler about repairing the Japanese lantern. "We found the string of pearls in the bottom."

Mr. Peters was astonished. "You'd better report the whole thing to the police at once," he advised. "I'll put the necklace in this box. Be very careful not to lose it on the way home."

The children eagerly discussed the mystery

as they walked back to the Mortons' house.

"Just think," said Honey Bunch, "maybe there were pearls in all those lanterns Mr. Kitts took!"

"Mr. Kitts must be very rich," Aniko observed. "And Norman is rich, too, with all that gold."

"What gold?" Norman asked, looking startled. "Why does everybody think I have gold?"

"Mrs. Miller told me," Honey Bunch said as she gave a little skip.

"Wh—?" Norman began, but at that moment the town rescue squad truck whizzed by them, its siren screaming.

"I wonder where it's going!" Norman shouted. "Let's follow it!"

He began to run so suddenly that he bumped into Honey Bunch. The little girl almost fell but recovered her footing. The four children raced on down the street. "Oh!" Honey Bunch exclaimed. "The rescue truck is stopping at our house!"

The children ran faster. In front of the Mortons' house they met Officer Reilly who had dashed up from the opposite direction.

"What happened, Honey Bunch?" he asked. "Is someone hurt?"

"I don't know!" she wailed.

They could see the driver of the rescue car talking to Mrs. Miller at the front door.

Honey Bunch ran up the walk. "What's the matter, Mrs. Miller?" she cried anxiously.

The kindly woman stopped and put her arms around the little girl. "No one's hurt, dear," she said. "But I had a scare."

"What was it, Mrs. Miller?" Norman asked.

Mrs. Miller dropped into a porch chair and began to fan herself with her apron. The rescue squad leader and Policeman Reilly listened intently while she told her story.

"I had finished putting away the laundry upstairs and was just coming down the back way when I saw a strange man standing in the kitchen," she began.

Officer Reilly whipped out his notebook. "What did the man look like?" he asked briskly, his pencil poised.

"He had his back to me," Mrs. Miller replied. "I couldn't see his face, but he wasn't very tall and his hair was black."

"Go on," the policeman urged.

"I guess he heard me coming down the stairs because he ran out the back door, jumped the fence, and went through the Clarks' yard onto the next street," Mrs. Miller explained.

68

"What did you do then?" Policeman Reilly asked.

Mrs. Miller looked embarrassed. "Well, Mrs. Morton had gone out, so I couldn't tell her. I was so excited, I just picked up the telephone receiver, dialed the operator, and yelled, 'Help!'"

"That's why I came," the rescue car driver said. "The telephone operator notified us that someone at this address needed help. Then I guess she called the police, too."

At that moment a squad car pulled up in front of the house and two men got out. Officer Reilly addressed them as Detective Dunn and Detective Gross and made his report.

"We'll have a look around the neighborhood," Detective Dunn said. "Perhaps we can pick up this fellow." He and Detective Gross got back into the squad car and drove off.

"I'll be on my way, too," the rescue man said.

Honey Bunch looked at Mr. Reilly. "I think I know who the man is that was in our house."

"Who?"

"His name is Mr. Kitts, and he was hunting for the broken paper lantern," Honey Bunch replied.

In answer to the policeman's questions, the

little girl told him about Mr. Kitts taking the Japanese paper lanterns away from her party and his insistence on finding the missing one.

"We found the lantern," Honey Bunch went on. "It was broken. After we fixed it, the pearls fell out of the false bottom. Here they are," she said. Reaching into the pocket of her shorts, she pulled out the white box and took off the top.

"Honey Bunch!" Norman cried. "The box is empty!"

Startled, Honey Bunch looked down. It was true. The pearls were gone! She felt in her pocket. The string of beads was not there.

"They must have fallen out when I bumped into you, Honey Bunch," Norman said ruefully.

"Let's go back and look for them!" Nikkio cried.

The four children hurried off the porch and began to run down the street.

"Don't go so fast!" Officer Reilly called as he followed them. "You'll have more chance of finding the pearls if you're not in such a hurry!"

When the policeman caught up with them, the children were moving along slowly, peering on each side of the walk.

Suddenly Norman cried out, "Look!"

The string of pearls dangled from a branch near the bottom of a hedge.

"Good for you, Norman!" Officer Reilly praised him. "You have sharp eyes! Now I think we'd better take these pearls right to Headquarters and you can tell the whole story to Captain Poston."

They retraced their steps to the Mortons' home where Officer Reilly put in a call for a police car. When it came, Honey Bunch and Norman, with Aniko and Nikkio, climbed in.

As soon as they arrived at Police Headquarters they were ushered into Captain Poston's private office. He was a tall, gray-haired man with a pleasant smile.

"Start from the beginning, children," he advised, "and tell me all about it."

Honey Bunch and Norman and their Japanese friends took turns telling the story of the two shipments of paper lanterns; how Mr. Kitts had claimed the extra carton; and of the discovery of the pearls.

Captain Poston leaned forward in his chair. "This is all very interesting," he commented. "You say you know where this Mr. Kitts lives?"

"Yes, sir," Norman spoke up. "I heard him say he lives at 64 Oak Street."

"Good," the captain said. "I'll have him brought in for questioning. My men will take you children home now. If I need you to identify Mr. Kitts, or give me any more information, I'll get in touch with you. In the meantime we'll keep the pearls in the police safe."

Captain Poston got up and walked toward the door with the children. As he opened it, he put one hand on Honey Bunch's shoulder and said mysteriously:

"Little girl, I won't know until tomorrow, but I think you've made a great discovery!"

CHAPTER VII

LITTLE JOKERS

NEXT morning Honey Bunch was still wondering what her great discovery was. She had just finished breakfast when the telephone rang. Mrs. Miller answered it and then came into the dining room.

"It's Captain Poston," she said. "He wants to talk to you, Honey Bunch."

Honey Bunch hastily slid from her chair and went to the telephone.

"Good morning," the police captain said. "I wonder if you and your little friends can come down to headquarters this morning. I'd like you to look at some pictures here and see if you can pick out Kitts."

"Wasn't he at 64 Oak Street?" Honey Bunch wanted to know.

"No," Captain Poston answered. "Nobody by that name has ever lived in that house. The man must have given you the wrong address."

73

"Captain Poston," Honey Bunch said. "May I ask you a question?"

"Why, of course," the genial officer replied.

"Can you tell me now what my important discovery is?"

"I certainly can," Captain Poston said. "Government police are looking for some men who have been bringing pearls into our country from Japan that they weren't supposed to. It's very possible that you've given us a good idea who one of them is."

"You mean maybe Mr. Kitts is a bad man!" Honey Bunch exclaimed. "I'll call Norman and Aniko and Nick. I know they'll want to come to the station with me."

"Fine," the captain remarked. "I'll send a police car around for you children in about half an hour."

When Honey Bunch told the other children about her call from Captain Poston they were all eager to go to police headquarters. Detective Gross picked them up and soon they were looking at books of pictures of people wanted by the police.

They turned over page after page with no luck, then Norman called out, "Here's Mr. Kitts!"

He held up the photograph of a bald-headed man with a long white beard!

Honey Bunch and the Japanese children giggled, but soon turned serious again and the search went on. Suddenly Aniko held up another picture. "Isn't this Mr. Kitts?" she asked.

The other children agreed that it was. Captain Poston read the description of the dark-haired man. His name was Skibben.

"I see he has the nickname of 'Nip' because he lived for some time in Nippon, which is another name for Japan," the captain continued. "It was Skibben who came to your house, Honey Bunch. I'll send out an alarm for him, although the chances are that he has left town by now."

Norman spoke up. "Remember that man who asked us about a Japanese family on Grove Street the other day, Honey Bunch?"

Honey Bunch nodded.

"Do you suppose he has anything to do with Mr. Kitts?"

Captain Poston had listened with interest. "What's this?" he put in. "Another suspect? Maybe you can find his picture here, too."

So Honey Bunch and Norman looked through the files again. This time Honey

Bunch spotted the mysterious blond stranger with the blinking eyes.

"Oho!" the captain exclaimed. "Now we really have something! That man is Claude Dibert. He's another bad man who is bringing jewels into our country. He has spent a good many years in Japan, too. His nickname is Blinky."

Honey Bunch thought very hard. "I wonder," she said, "if he knows anything about Honey Blossom's secret."

When Captain Poston asked what the little girl meant, she told him about finding the note in the carton of tea cups from Tokyo.

"I'll get in touch with the Tokyo police," the captain said. "This secret might possibly have something to do with those men. We don't want to overlook any clue."

Captain Poston thanked Honey Bunch and her friends for their great help. Then Detective Gross drove the children home.

Honey Bunch ran into her house. "Mother! Mrs. Miller!" she called. "Did I get a letter from Honey Blossom?"

"Not yet, dear," her mother replied. "I'm afraid you'll have to wait a few days more. Japan is a long way from here, you know."

At lunch, Honey Bunch said to her mother, "I'm worried about the Kito family. Do you think those bad men might try to harm them because they received the box of paper lanterns by mistake?"

Mrs. Morton did not wish to alarm Honey Bunch, but this was what she had been thinking. Finally she suggested, "Why don't you talk to Captain Poston about it?"

Honey Bunch ran to the telephone and soon had the police officer on the line. After she had told him her fears, the captain said, "I'm glad you mentioned it, Honey Bunch. If the Kitos don't object, I'll put a guard at their home for a few nights."

Honey Bunch thanked him. Then Captain Poston added, "By the way, I'm expecting to hear from the Tokyo police soon. I'll let you know if they have any news on Honey Blossom."

That afternoon Honey Bunch and Norman went down the street to play with Aniko and Nikkio.

Mrs. Kito greeted them, then announced, "Captain Poston called, and offered to send a guard here. I am relieved. I, too, have worried about this lantern business."

Norman was excited at the prospect of a police guard being stationed right in the neighborhood. "Oh boy!" he burst out. "I wish I could help him catch the bad men!"

"Maybe we will," Honey Bunch said wisely. Then she turned to Mrs. Kito. "May Aniko stay overnight at my house? Mother would like to have her."

"And my mother said Nick could stay with me," Norman joined in.

"Oh, may we, Mama-san?" Aniko asked, her black eyes shining with happiness.

Mrs. Kito agreed with a smile. The Japanese children ran to pack their overnight things. They returned, each carrying a package wrapped in a gaily printed piece of cloth.

"How pretty!" Honey Bunch exclaimed.

"These are *furoshiki*," Aniko said. "Japanese people like to carry their belongings in a square of cloth rather than in bags."

The children held up the furoshiki for Honey Bunch and Norman to see. The yellow one containing Aniko's things was printed with a picture of beautiful Mt. Fuji. Nikkio's was blue. On it was pictured a black-and-white bird standing on one long, thin leg.

"That's a crane," Nikkio explained proudly. "They are very popular in Japan."

Norman held one foot in his hand and began

to hop around on the other. "See! I'm a **crane!**" he cried. He hopped out the front door toward the steps leading to the sidewalk.

But as he approached the top step Norman gave too big a hop. He missed the step and sprawled headlong to the ground!

As the others gasped, he sat up quickly. "I'm all right," he announced cheerfully. "I just bumped my head a little."

Mrs. Kito ran to the kitchen and returned with several ice cubes wrapped in a cloth. "Here, Norman," she said. "Hold this on your head. By the time you get home, the bump won't hurt at all."

A little later, Norman and Nikkio turned off Grove Street to go to the Clarks' house. The girls waved good-by and went into Honey Bunch's home.

After Aniko had bowed prettily to Mrs. Morton, she thanked her for the invitation. Then Honey Bunch said, "Come on upstairs, Aniko. I'll show you my room."

When the girls entered Honey Bunch's bedroom, Aniko admired the twin beds with their pretty ruffled spreads. "It will be funny to sleep so far up from the floor!" she exclaimed with a little laugh.

Just then there came a little scratching noise

from the clothes closet. "Oh dear!" Honey Bunch cried. "I'm afraid Lady Clare—she's my cat—has been shut in there!"

She ran to the closet and threw open the door. "Come—" she began. Then she let out a shriek.

A white-covered figure sprang at her!

Before Honey Bunch could move, the white covering was flung off and there stood a girl. Her cousin Stub!

"Oh!" cried Honey Bunch.

Stub's real name was Mary, but everyone called her Stub because she was always stubbing her toe. Her parents were Mr. Morton's brother Rand and his wife Carol. They lived on a farm about an hour's drive from Barham.

"Stub! I'm glad to see you even if you did scare me!" Honey Bunch threw her arms about her cousin and they danced around. The girls always did this when they had not seen each other for a while.

Honey Bunch introduced Stub to Aniko. Then she exclaimed, "You two look sort of like each other."

Stub Morton, like Aniko, had black bobbed hair and sparkling dark eyes. She was just a little taller than Aniko.

"I hope I can bunk in here with you girls," Stub said. "We'll have fun!"

A white-covered figure sprang at her!

Later, when it was time to go to bed, Mr. Morton brought in a cot for Stub to sleep on. The little girls climbed into their beds, but it was a long time before they fell asleep. Stub kept the others laughing with her stories about the animals on the farm. Honey Bunch told her cousin about finding the pearls in the Japanese paper lantern.

Finally, Mrs. Morton called, "Girls, please stop talking now and go to sleep."

So they settled down and in a few minutes were fast asleep. Some time later Honey Bunch awoke. Bright moonlight filled the room. She looked over at the other bed. It was empty!

"I wonder where Aniko is," she thought. "Perhaps she's gone for a drink of water."

Honey Bunch waited for a few minutes but the little Japanese girl did not return. Then she called, "Stub! Stub!"

Her cousin sat up in bed. "What's the matter, Honey Bunch?" she whispered.

"Aniko is gone!" the little girl replied. "Where do you s'pose she is?"

Stub jumped up from the cot and started toward Honey Bunch's bed. Suddenly she stopped and began to giggle. "Here she is!"

82

Stub pointed to the floor between the twin beds. There lay Aniko sound asleep on a blanket!

"I guess she likes it better there 'cause she's used to sleeping on futons," Honey Bunch explained to Stub as her cousin climbed back into bed.

It seemed to Honey Bunch just a few minutes later when she woke again. But this time the room was full of light. One little sunbeam pranced around the wall.

"That's funny," Honey Bunch thought. "I never saw a sunbeam like that before!"

While she lay watching it, the ray suddenly settled on Stub's face. The farm girl sat up, rubbing her eyes. "Wh—" she began, but as she spoke the little beam danced over to Honey Bunch's bed.

"That's not a real sunbeam!" Stub exclaimed and ran to the window. Honey Bunch followed her.

By this time Aniko, too, had awakened. When the little Japanese girl recalled where she had been sleeping she giggled. "So sorry," she murmured, then ran to the window with the other girls.

"It's Norman!" Honey Bunch cried.

At an upstairs window of the Clarks' house

stood Norman and Nikkio. They had a little mirror which they were taking turns shining into Honey Bunch's room!

The girls waved to the two boys, then dressed and went downstairs to breakfast. When the meal was over, Stub suggested that they play a trick on Norman and Nikkio.

"All right," Honey Bunch agreed. "What shall we do?"

Stub told Honey Bunch and Aniko what she had in mind and they agreed in delight. The three little girls hurried up to Honey Bunch's room. Quickly Stub and Aniko changed dresses with each other.

"Now make me look Japanese," Stub directed.

"I think your bangs should be shorter," Aniko suggested.

Honey Bunch got some blunt-end scissors which she used for cutting out paper dolls and carefully trimmed the ends of Stub's black bangs.

Stub looked at herself in the mirror. "I still don't look like Aniko," she remarked sadly.

"I know!" Honey Bunch ran from the room and came back with a little make-up kit which

Mrs. Morton sometimes carried when she went on a trip.

Honey Bunch then covered Stub's rosy cheeks with pale face powder. Next Aniko picked up the black eyebrow pencil and drew arches into the little girl's straight brows.

Stub examined herself in the mirror again. "That's better!" she cried. She took the pencil and drew straight lines upward from the ends of her eyelids.

Just then the girls heard Norman at the back door asking Mrs. Miller if Honey Bunch and Aniko could come outside. A moment later, Honey Bunch and Stub, giggling, hurried downstairs.

"Come on out, Aniko!" Honey Bunch called as she ran into the back yard where the boys were waiting.

When Stub, dressed as Aniko, walked out the door, Nikkio stared at her in horror. "Oh, Aniko," he cried, "something has happened to you! I will tell Mama-san!"

With that, he dashed toward the street.

CHAPTER VIII

PEARL DIVING

"NICK! Come back!" Honey Bunch called after the Japanese boy.

Nikkio stopped and turned around, uncertain. The real Aniko came out of the house. She walked down the driveway and took her brother's hand.

"It is just a joke, Nikkio," she explained. "This girl is Stub, Honey Bunch's cousin."

When the little boy saw the two girls together, he grinned. "I thought you had changed while you were asleep," he said sheepishly.

Norman was very glad to see Stub. She was a tomboy and just as good at games as he was.

"You look awful funny with that stuff on your face." He laughed loudly.

Stub laughed too, and said, "That'll teach you to shine mirrors at us." Then she and Aniko went into the house and changed back into their own clothes. Stub scrubbed her face and came back with every freckle showing prominently.

The Japanese children went home and a little later Honey Bunch, Stub, and Norman set off together for Sunday-school. Early Monday morning Aniko, Nikkio, and Norman came back to Honey Bunch's yard.

"What shall we play?" Norman asked. He thrust his hands deep into the pockets of his shorts and began to jingle a few coins.

"Why, Norman," Honey Bunch exclaimed, "Mrs. Miller told me you had quiet gold!"

Norman looked completely bewildered. "I don't know what you're talking about, Honey Bunch. What *do* you mean, anyhow?"

But before the little girl could explain, Mrs. Miller called her to the telephone. When Honey Bunch came into the yard again she was smiling.

"That was Ida Camp," she explained. "She has a big new play swimming pool in her yard and wants us all to come over."

"Pollywogs!" Norman cried. "That's great! Come on, Nick. We'll go put on some trunks!"

The little Japanese boy's white teeth showed in a wide grin as he followed his new friend over the fence.

Honey Bunch gave Stub and Aniko each a bathing suit and in a few minutes the five children were running down Grove Street toward the Camps' house.

"How scrumptious!" Honey Bunch exclaimed when she saw the pool. It was round, about fifteen feet across and three feet deep. The water sparkled in the sunlight.

"There are some masks and playthings to use in the water," Ida said proudly, pointing out bright-colored balls, rubber rings, and mechanical boats.

"I'll be a pearl diver!" Norman shouted. He picked up a diving mask and slipped it on his head. Then he climbed over the side of the pool and dropped into it with a great splash!

Stub winked at the other children and walked over to the driveway. She picked up a handful of white pebbles and with them in her hand she, too, climbed into the pool. In a few minutes all the children were splashing merrily in the cool water.

Norman continued his "pearl diving." Suddenly he gave a shout. "I've found some pearls!" He ducked his head and came up with a handful of white stones.

The other children began to giggle. Stub

laughed so hard that she fell over backward and sat down in the water. She scrambled to her feet and stood shaking water from her eyes. "Help!" she cried, "I'm drowning!"

With a grin, Norman tucked the stones into the pocket of his trunks. "All right, Stub," he cried. "It serves you right for fooling me!"

At that moment Mr. Reilly, Honey Bunch's puppy, raced into the yard. With a great leap

he jumped into the pool! He paddled furiously, swimming around the edge.

"Mr. Reilly," Honey Bunch scolded him, "you're not supposed to be in this pool!"

"I'll get him out," Norman volunteered. He caught the slippery puppy in his arms and tried to lift him over the side of the pool. But the squirming dog was too much for him. Norman lost his balance and he, too, sat down in the water!

This time it was Stub's turn to laugh. "I'll help you, Norman," she said, and pulled the boy to his feet. Together they lifted Mr. Reilly out onto the grass.

"Oh!" came a startled cry. Mrs. Camp had come up to the pool just as Mr. Reilly began to shake himself vigorously. She was showered with flying drops of water!

Honey Bunch scrambled out of the pool. "I'm sorry, Mrs. Camp! Mr. Reilly is a naughty puppy!"

Mrs. Camp laughed. "No harm done. I just came to tell you, Honey Bunch, that your mother called. She has a message for you from Captain Poston at police headquarters."

"Oh, goody!" Honey Bunch exclaimed. "I'll dry myself with a towel and go find out what it is."

Stub and Norman said they would join her.
Aniko and Nikkio decided to stay and play in
the pool for a little while.

A few minutes later Honey Bunch called,
"Here I am, Mother!" as she, Stub, and Norman ran into her house.

Mrs. Morton told them that Captain Poston
had heard from the Tokyo police. So far they
had not been able to locate any of the people in
Japan who were working with Mr. Kitts or
Blinky. They had, however, learned something
about Honey Blossom. Her father was a
packer in the factory from which Mr. Kito had
ordered the tea cups. He apparently had no
connection with the paper lanterns. None of
the family knew where their cousin Henry was.

"We'll find him!" Honey Bunch declared.
"And if the police in Tokyo can't find the bad
men," the little girl remarked, "we'll have to
find some more clues here!"

"Let's start looking right away," Norman
urged and ran home.

Honey Bunch and Stub hurried to put on
their shorts and blouses. Presently they heard
Norman shout:

"Honey Bunch and Stub! I've found some
footprints! Come out and see!"

The girls dashed into the back yard. There,

placed at intervals on the grass, were pieces of brown wrapping paper. They were cut in the shape of footprints!

Honey Bunch and Stub laughed but then Honey Bunch scolded, "Norman, you mustn't keep playing tricks, if we're really going to catch the bad men!"

Norman promised to search for clues in earnest. At that moment Mrs. Miller called from the back door, "Honey Bunch, you have a visitor!"

"Who is it?" the little girl asked.

Mrs. Miller smiled mysteriously and did not answer. So Honey Bunch, followed closely by Stub and Norman, ran into the living room. There in a big chair sat a handsome young man with twinkling blue eyes.

"Flyer Frank!" Honey Bunch cried. She ran across the room and threw herself in his arms. "I'm so happy to see you!"

Stub and Norman also greeted the pilot with enthusiasm. He was a great favorite of the children, who all called him Flyer Frank, though his real name was Mr. Franklin.

"And what have you three been doing?" the young man asked, rumpling Norman's hair.

"We're looking for bad men!" Honey Bunch

told him excitedly. "They brought pearls into our country they weren't supposed to!"

"Smugglers!" Flyer Frank exclaimed in amazement. "Let's hear all about them."

Honey Bunch and Norman took turns explaining how they had discovered the string of cultured pearls in the false base of the Japanese lantern. They also told Flyer Frank about Mr. Kitts and the inquisitive stranger who had turned out to be "Blinky" Dibert.

"Say!" Flyer Frank said. "That 'Blinky' fellow sounds like the one I heard about yesterday!"

"What do you mean?" Honey Bunch asked eagerly.

"My friend, Ted Steel, was telling me last night about a passenger he flew down to Wellsburg in his little two-seater. He said this man blinked his eyes all the time."

"Maybe it's the same one we saw!" Norman put in.

"He did something else strange," Flyer Frank continued, "but Ted was interrupted and I didn't hear the whole story."

"I wish I could talk to him." Honey Bunch said with a sigh.

"Why not?" the flyer remarked. "Ted was to

be at the airport today. I can drive you there."

"Oh, would you?" Honey Bunch exclaimed.

Mrs. Morton had gone out, but Mrs. Miller gave her consent to the trip. The three children piled into Flyer Frank's sports car and drove to the small airport on the outskirts of Barham.

They found Ted Steel in the pilots' lounge. He was a stocky, blond young man with a pleasant smile. Flyer Frank introduced the children then said:

"Honey Bunch would like to talk to you about that strange passenger you had yesterday."

"You mean the one who blinked his eyes so often?" Ted Steel asked.

"Yes," Honey Bunch spoke up. "Do you know his name?"

"Well, he said it was Sims, but I noticed his wallet had the initial D on it," the flyer replied.

"It must have been Mr. Dibert!" Norman burst out.

"Did Mr. Sims have suitcases with him?" Honey Bunch asked.

"No. But he did have a carton which he insisted upon holding on his lap during the entire trip. I wanted him to put it behind him on the floor but he refused."

"The paper lanterns!" Honey Bunch cried excitedly.

When she noticed that Ted Steel looked puzzled, she told him the story of the mysterious Japanese lanterns.

"Did Mr. Sims say where he was going in Wellsburg?" Honey Bunch said.

"No, he didn't. But if anyone was expecting that package, he never got it!" the pilot replied.

"Why not?" asked Norman.

"Just as we were beginning the approach to the Wellsburg airport, Mr. Sims opened the window next to him and dumped out the carton!"

"Dumped it!" Stub exclaimed. "Why would he do that?"

"I asked him, but he refused to answer," the pilot said. "Personally, I think it was because of the plane behind us."

"What plane was that?" Flyer Frank asked.

"Another plane seemed to be following us," Ted Steel explained. "This fellow Sims kept looking back as if he was very worried."

Honey Bunch's blue eyes grew very wide. "I'm sure there were more pearls in the package. He was afraid somebody in the other plane was going to catch him. We must find Blinky!"

CHAPTER IX

A MUD-STUCK PLANE

"YES!" Stub agreed with Honey Bunch. "We must find Blinky." Then she asked Ted Steel, "Do you know who was in the plane behind you?"

The pilot shook his head. "I wish I did. At the time I didn't have any reason to pay special attention to it."

"Pollywogs!" Norman exclaimed. "Maybe the police were chasing Blinky in that plane!"

Honey Bunch had another idea. "Maybe he dropped the carton so a friend of his could pick it up," she suggested.

"Perhaps. But the land is very wooded near the Wellsburg airport," Ted Steel observed. "I should think the package would be difficult to find."

Honey Bunch thanked Flyer Frank's friend for his help.

"That's all right," he said pleasantly. "If I

find out anything else about Blinky, I'll let you know."

On the way home Flyer Frank drove past the corner where Officer Reilly was on duty. The policeman waved when he saw Honey Bunch.

"Oh please, Flyer Frank!" the little girl cried. "Will you stop? I want to speak to Mr. Reilly."

Flyer Frank pulled over to the curb and the officer walked up to them. Excitedly Honey Bunch told him about their call on Ted Steel and the story of his peculiar passenger. "We're sure it was Blinky Dibert," she said.

Officer Reilly took off his hat and rubbed his head. "That's valuable information," he said. "I'll pass it on to Captain Poston right away."

Then he smiled. "You know, Honey Bunch, there's talk of promoting me to detective. I'm sure it's because of all the help you've given me on this pearl case."

"That's wonderful, Mr. Reilly!" Honey Bunch exclaimed, her eyes shining.

"But then you wouldn't be on this corner any more!" Norman said mournfully.

"That's right," Officer Reilly agreed. "Well, we'll see what happens."

When Flyer Frank and the children reached

the Mortons' home and went into the living room they saw a slim, dark-haired woman talking to Honey Bunch's mother.

"Mother!" Stub exclaimed. "I didn't know you were coming today!"

"Aunt Carol! Can you stay a while?" Honey Bunch cried, running over to hug her pretty aunt.

The woman smiled and shook her head. Honey Bunch introduced Flyer Frank. Then her mother said, "I've been trying to persuade Aunt Carol at least to stay to dinner, but she says she and Stub must leave."

"But I want to stay and help solve the mystery of the paper lantern," the tomboy pleaded.

Aunt Carol explained that she, Uncle Rand, and their daughter were going on a little trip in a few days and must go home to get ready.

"I'll write to you, Stub," Honey Bunch promised, "and tell you everything that happens."

"And come back soon, Stub," Norman called as the little girl and her mother walked to their car.

Back in the house again, Honey Bunch told Mrs. Morton all about the clue they had picked up from Ted Steel.

When she finished, Flyer Frank spoke up. "If you like, Honey Bunch, we could fly over the area near the Wellsburg airport and look for any signs of that carton."

"Oh, that would be wonderful! May we, Mother?" the little girl cried.

"Why don't you stay to dinner, Frank," Mrs. Morton replied, "and we'll see what Mr. Morton thinks of the idea."

Norman drew Honey Bunch aside. "If you go, will you take me with you?" he whispered.

"Of course, Norman," his playmate answered. "I'll let you know what Daddy says."

That evening while they enjoyed one of Mrs. Miller's special fried-chicken dinners, Mr. Morton was brought up to date on the story of Blinky and the paper lanterns.

"We think the lanterns were in the carton which Blinky threw out of Ted Steel's plane," Honey Bunch added. "And Flyer Frank says he'll fly me over to look for them. Please, Daddy, may Norman and I go?"

"What do you think, David?" Mrs. Morton asked.

"I see no objection if Frank is willing," Mr. Morton replied. "Why don't you go along, too, Edith?"

"Oh, yes, Mother! Please come!"

Honey Bunch begged Mrs. Morton who smilingly agreed to accompany the children on the sleuthing trip. When Flyer Frank left a short while later he promised to meet his passengers at the airport at nine-thirty the next morning. Honey Bunch telephoned Norman.

"I'll be ready!" her playmate said excitedly.

Next morning, directly after breakfast, Honey Bunch ran out to the back yard. "Norman!" she called.

Immediately a dark head popped up over the fence top. "I've been waiting for you, Honey Bunch," Norman said. "When are we leaving?"

"Right now," the little girl said. "Hurry!"

In a twinkling Norman was over the fence. Mrs. Morton came out and the three climbed into her car.

Promptly at nine-thirty Mrs. Morton and the two children drove up to the Barham airport building. Flyer Frank was waiting and led them out to the field where his trim plane was parked.

They got in and he taxied out onto the runway. At a signal from the control tower, he gunned the motor and sped down the runway. In another minute they were flying over Barham Park on the way to Wellsburg.

"There's where you sailed your umbrella boat!" Honey Bunch teased Norman.

He grinned sheepishly and changed the subject. "Look at all the little tiny cars down there." He pointed below.

When they had flown for about fifteen minutes Flyer Frank began to look uneasy. "We're running into a storm," he observed.

The sky had grown steadily darker and in another minute the rain began to come down in sheets. There were bright flashes of lightning and loud claps of thunder.

Flyer Frank turned to Mrs. Morton. "I think I'd better put down," he said. "I'm watching for a solid-looking field."

Mrs. Morton nodded and peered anxiously out the window. The children did the same, as the rain continued to beat furiously against the plane.

"I'm going down there." Flyer Frank pointed to a green field off to the left. He flew over it, then circled and came in for a landing. The landscape rushed by them and then with a little bump they were down!

"Pollywogs!" Norman cried. "You're a keen pilot, Flyer Frank!"

The young man grinned. "We'll just sit here until the storm blows over," he said. "Then I can take off again."

They all felt safe and cozy in the plane as the

storm raged outside. Gradually the wind stopped howling and the rain slackened to a gentle drizzle. Then it stopped and the sun broke through the clouds and shone brightly.

"We can go on now," Flyer Frank said. "The storm's over." He pushed the starter button. The engine sprang to life. The plane shuddered, but did not move forward.

"I think we're stuck," the pilot remarked. He opened the door and hopped down to the grass.

The heavy rain had softened the field to such an extent that the wheels of the plane had sunk into the muddy ground. The power of the engine was not enough to move them.

"Oh dear!" Honey Bunch sighed. "How will we get to Wellsburg today?"

"Here comes somebody!" Norman cried. "There's a girl on horseback riding out of those woods."

They all watched as the rider came nearer. Then Honey Bunch exclaimed, "It's Stub!"

Norman leaned out the window. "Hey, Stub!" he shouted. "Come rescue us!"

"What are you doing here, Stub?" Mrs. Morton asked as the girl rode her horse up to the stranded plane.

"This is part of our farm now," Stub explained. "Daddy bought it a couple of days ago for pasture. I heard your plane come down."

The farm girl volunteered to go for help. "I'll go get Daddy and he can pull you out with the tractor."

She rode off and a short while later the group saw Uncle Rand Morton coming across the field on a tractor. Stub had abandoned her horse and now rode on her father's lap.

"Well, hello everybody," the ruddy-faced farmer called jovially as he came up to the plane. "This is a new way to pay us a visit!"

They exchanged greetings and Flyer Frank explained their predicament to Mr. Morton.

"Do you think you can pull us out, Rand?" Mrs. Morton asked anxiously.

"I think so, Edith—in just a few shakes," her brother-in-law answered.

Uncle Rand brought a rope from the tractor and fastened it to the plane. The pilot climbed back into his seat.

Uncle Rand started the tractor moving across the field. The rope grew taut. Suddenly the plane gave a jerk as it sprang from the mud.

Honey Bunch giggled. "This is the first time I've ever been in a plane which had to be towed!" she said. Norman laughed, too.

The ride was rather bumpy but before long Uncle Rand pulled the plane into the barnyard. Aunt Carol ran out of the farmhouse and greeted the passengers warmly as they stepped to the ground.

"Come into the house," she urged. "You must need a little refreshment."

In a short time they were seated around the table in the big dining room. Aunt Carol brought in steaming cups of coffee for Honey

Bunch's mother and Flyer Frank, while the three children had cocoa and ginger cookies.

"I think I'll call Mrs. Miller," Mrs. Morton said, after she had finished her coffee. "She might be worrying about us."

When she returned from the telephone, she had an odd expression on her face. Honey Bunch noticed it at once.

"What's the matter, Mother?" she asked. "What did Mrs. Miller say?"

Mrs. Morton smiled. "It seems you're on the right track of your mystery. Mrs. Miller says Officer Reilly stopped at the house this morning. He told her that he had received a report that both Nip Skibben and Blinky Dibert had been seen around Wellsburg!"

"Yippee!" Norman cried. He jumped up from his chair, dashed into the living room, and began to play Chopsticks on the piano. Norman always did this when he was particularly pleased or excited.

"We'd better hurry to Wellsburg," Honey Bunch said anxiously.

"Think you can take off from the yard, Frank?" Farmer Morton asked. He seemed worried.

Flyer Frank shook his head. "I'm afraid a take-off on this soggy ground might be danger-

105

ous. I'll have to leave the plane here until evening when the earth will be drier."

"Why can't we take off from the super highway?" Norman asked.

Flyer Frank looked at Mr. Morton. "That's a good idea. Do you think it would be allowed?"

"I'll call the State Police," the farmer offered. "I'm sure that as soon as they find out the circumstances they'll give you permission."

When Uncle Rand returned from the telephone he said that State Troopers would meet the plane at the super highway and arrange for the take-off.

The wide road ran near the end of the farm lane and it was a matter of only minutes for the plane to be towed there. The pilot, Mrs. Morton, Honey Bunch, and Norman took their places. Then the State Trooper in charge called up to Flyer Frank:

"We've stopped traffic a mile in each direction. Will that be enough?"

The flyer made a circle with his thumb and forefinger and nodded. "Roger!" he replied.

The plane was turned to face into the wind. Flyer Frank started the motor and the aircraft rushed up the highway!

CHAPTER X

LOST!

HONEY BUNCH and Norman held their breaths as the plane sped along the highway.

"Whee!" Norman cried. "If the other kids could only see us now!"

Honey Bunch giggled. "Elmer Gray will never believe we rode up the street in a plane!"

At this moment the craft rose into the air over the line of stopped cars. Honey Bunch and Norman opened the window on one side. They leaned out and waved to the startled drivers.

The plane rose higher and soon the automobiles on the road below looked like beetles scurrying along a track.

Half an hour later, Flyer Frank announced, "We're getting near Wellsburg."

"There are the woods!" Honey Bunch pointed out. "That must be where Blinky threw the carton overboard."

The pilot came down as low as he dared and

circled the patch of woodland. The occupants of the plane peered from the windows at the ground below.

"The trees are too thick," Honey Bunch observed. "We won't be able to see the carton from the air."

"Might as well land at the Wellsburg field," Flyer Frank said. "I know the airport manager. Perhaps he can tell us something more about the mysterious Blinky."

The pilot received a signal from the control tower to come in, and set the plane down near the small airport building. A heavy-set man with a jolly smile walked out onto the field.

"I thought that was your plane, Frank," he said. "What brings you to Wellsburg?"

Flyer Frank introduced his friend as Bob Wilson. He then explained their errand and described the passenger whom Ted Steel had brought to the airport two days before.

"I saw a man who looked like that hanging around the field this morning," Mr. Wilson said. "He was with another man. When one of our mechanics asked what they wanted, the two of them ran off into those woods over there."

"Let's chase 'em!" Norman cried excitedly.

"There's a garage right here where you can rent a car," Mr. Wilson told him.

"Good," Flyer Frank spoke up. He went to the garage but returned in a few minutes. "We'll have to wait until after lunch," he said.

The airport manager offered his car for a ride into town. "Try the Cup and Saucer Restaurant on Main Street," Bob Wilson advised. "They have good food."

It was a short ride. Flyer Frank drove along slowly, searching for a place to park.

"Oh look!" Honey Bunch suddenly cried. "There are some Japanese lanterns."

The car was just passing a place called the Oriental Shop. In the window were displayed three paper lanterns of different colors, but the same design.

"I wish we could go in," Honey Bunch said. "But we should look for Blinky's carton first, before he finds it."

"You bet," Norman agreed.

Finally Frank parked near the Cup and Saucer Restaurant. The visitors entered the attractive dining room. On the pale-blue wallpaper were printed white cups and saucers placed at all angles.

Norman walked over to one wall. Leaning far over, he said, grinning impishly, "I think I'll have to stand on my head to drink from this cup!"

Honey Bunch giggled. "You're silly, Norman!" she said.

They sat down at a table, then ordered sandwiches and milk shakes. As soon as they had finished, the children, eager to set out for the woods, led the way outside. They returned the borrowed car and picked up the rented one.

A little later Flyer Frank parked at the edge of the woods. Norman jumped out first and opened the door for Mrs. Morton and Honey Bunch. "This seems like a big woods," he said, looking worried.

"We'll go slowly and search very carefully," Flyer Frank advised.

The group walked in among the trees. Honey Bunch and Norman ran ahead along a little path. They peered under ferns and undergrowth. Several times chipmunks and squirrels scurried away at their approach.

After a while Honey Bunch stopped and turned around. With a surprised expression she said, "Norman, where are Mother and Flyer Frank?"

Norman looked blank. "I don't know," he admitted. "I thought they were right behind us."

There was no sign of the grownups and no

sound except the rustle of the leaves in the breeze.

"Oh, Norman, do you think we're lost?" Honey Bunch asked, her voice shaking a little.

"No," Norman said bravely, thrusting his hands deep into his pockets. "Let's call real loud, so they can hear us."

Honey Bunch and her playmate shouted several times at the top of their lungs. But there was no answer.

Although she felt very scared now, Honey Bunch was determined to act brave, too. "I guess we were so busy looking," she said, "we didn't notice which way we were going."

Both she and Norman thought very hard what to do next. Suddenly Norman exclaimed:

"I know what!" He pulled a handful of small white pebbles from his pocket. "I still have my pearls," he said with a grin. "I'll drop them as we go along and your mother and Flyer Frank can follow our trail."

"That's a wonderful idea, Norman!" Honey Bunch agreed. "That way we won't be lost any more!"

The two children walked on, carefully examining the ground. Every few feet Norman dropped one of the white stones.

Suddenly there came a thrashing noise from the bushes in front of them. The children halted. The next second a young deer dashed out of the thicket and sped past them in the opposite direction.

"Pollywogs!" Norman exclaimed. "He must be running away from something!"

Honey Bunch agreed. "He was so scared he didn't even see us!"

"What do you suppose scared the deer?" Norman asked in surprise.

"I don't know. But if we go in the direction he came from, maybe we'll find out," Honey Bunch proposed.

"Okay, let's be real quiet," Norman agreed.

The two children crept forward, being very careful not to make any noise. They had gone only a short distance when Honey Bunch, who was in front, held up her hand.

Norman joined her. Quickly they ducked behind a cluster of bushes. From the other side of the thicket came the sound of voices.

"I give up," a man announced. "The pearls aren't here. That pilot must have found 'em. He's messed things up for us plenty!"

Another voice spoke up. "I saw some nice pearls in Kito's store. What a nice wild duck he'd make!"

112

A young deer dashed out of the thicket

After that there was silence. Honey Bunch stealthily parted the bushes and peeked through the opening. The men were gone!

"Norman," she said, "I'm sure they were Nip and Blinky. I know their voices!"

"Do you think we should try to catch them?" Norman asked.

"We'd better wait for Flyer Frank," Honey Bunch advised. "I wish he and Mother would find us."

Norman suddenly turned and looked behind him. "Ssh!" he whispered. "I thought I heard someone talking back there!"

"Oh! Do you suppose those bad men have gone around behind us?" Honey Bunch shivered.

Norman did not answer but pulled his playmate behind a large tree.

Sure enough the children now distinctly heard voices. In another minute two figures stepped into view. "It's Mother and Flyer Frank!" Honey Bunch cried in relief, and ran to greet them.

"Oh thank goodness!" Mrs. Morton hugged her daughter, then Norman. "Are you all right?"

"Yes," Honey Bunch replied. "We won't get lost again."

"We found the trail of white stones," Flyer Frank added. "Did you children leave it?"

Norman modestly waited for Honey Bunch to explain. She did. "It was Norman's idea!" she announced.

"Done like a true explorer, Norman," Flyer Frank said. "We'd never have found you so quickly otherwise. But please don't run so far ahead of us next time."

Honey Bunch and Norman promised, then Honey Bunch excitedly told her mother and the pilot, "We heard Blinky and Nip talking. They were right behind those bushes." She pointed, and reported tthe conversation.

Mrs. Morton and Flyer Frank were amazed. "Which way did the men go?" asked the pilot.

The children had to admit they were not sure. "The bad men just seemed to disappear all of a sudden," Honey Bunch added.

Norman looked puzzled. "What did they mean when they called Mr. Kito a wild duck?"

Mrs. Morton and Flyer Frank shook their heads. "I think we'd better give up our search and report this to the police here," the pilot advised. "Evidently those men didn't find the carton either."

He and the others made their way out of the woods and back to the car. Flyer Frank drove

115

to police headquarters where Honey Bunch and Norman told their story to the captain.

The tall officer listened intently. When they had finished he exclaimed, "You children are very good detectives! Captain Poston has already told me about this Blinky Dibert who calls himself Sims, and that he dropped a suspicious package from the plane. So he and his pal Nip Skibben are still in the area."

"And I sure wish we could have caught them," Norman put in.

"Well, thanks to you children, they may be captured soon," the captain said. "I'll tell my men to be on the lookout for Nip, alias Mr. Kitts, and Blinky."

As the party left police headquarters Flyer Frank said, "Shall we go back and pick up the plane now?"

Honey Bunch had been quiet. Now she said, "Mother, I have an idea. Please, may we stay here overnight and search for the carton in the morning?"

"Why, Honey Bunch? Do you still think we can find the carton if those two men couldn't?" Mrs. Morton asked in surprise.

Honey Bunch nodded, her eyes sparkling. "That's part of my idea."

"Let's hear all about it!" Flyer Frank said.

CHAPTER XI

THE "MERRY WINDMILL"

"HURRY up, Honey Bunch!" Norman urged. "Tell us what your idea is."

"I think we should search in the tops of the trees for the carton!" Honey Bunch announced.

Norman looked astonished. "Why do you think the carton would be up there?" he asked.

The little girl explained that the package thrown from the plane might have struck the tree tops and broken open. Perhaps pieces of it had caught in the branches.

"I think you have a good thought, Honey Bunch!" Flyer Frank exclaimed. "It might be worth staying overnight, Mrs. Morton, so we can try out your daughter's idea."

Honey Bunch's mother looked thoughtful, then agreed, "All right. Is there a good motel nearby?"

The pilot assured her that there was and in a few minutes drove up in front of an attractive one-story building. It was called the Shadow-lawn Motel. Each unit had a tiny porch in front of the door and a little evergreen tree in a bright red pot.

"How pretty!" Honey Bunch exclaimed. "It'll be fun to stay here."

First Mrs. Morton telephoned Daddy Morton to let him know of the new plan. Then she called Mrs. Clark, who gave permission for Norman to stay. Flyer Frank went to the office and arranged for rooms.

"You and I will bunk together, pardner," he said to Norman, rumpling the little boy's black hair.

Norman grinned and turned a cart wheel on the smooth green lawn. Honey Bunch and her mother went into the cozy room assigned to them. By the time they had freshened up supper was being served.

The four enjoyed a delicious meal in the coffee shop attached to the motel. Then they strolled up the main street of the town. "We'll have to buy ourselves some night things," Mrs. Morton reminded the others.

The children enjoyed picking out what they needed in the small dry-goods store. Norman chose bright red-and-white striped pajamas,

118

while Honey Bunch decided on blue ones printed with little pink parasols. "They make me think of Aniko," she explained.

When they came out of the shop Honey Bunch noticed that the Oriental Shop they had seen earlier in the day was next door. It was open. "May we go in and look around, Mother?" she asked. "I want to see those paper lanterns."

Mrs. Morton agreed and they walked into the shop. The visitors were met not by an Oriental, but by an American man. He was rather fierce looking and the children disliked him at once.

He was of medium height and heavy. His oily hair was parted in the middle and slicked back. It was so long that it curled around his ears.

"Are you looking for anything special?" he asked Mrs. Morton in a hoarse voice.

Honey Bunch spoke up. "May I please see one of the Japanese lanterns you have in the window?" she asked.

"Of course. Nice, eh? Just came in from Tokyo." He hurried over to the window and came back holding one of the lanterns.

Honey Bunch took the paper globe and turned it in her hand. The lantern had the same design as the one which Norman had

119

broken! The round black piece at the bottom was even covered exactly as the other had been!

"I wonder if there's anything inside this one," she mused. Cautiously she held the lantern to her ear and shook it. She heard nothing.

But as she examined the lantern Flyer Frank noticed that the clerk was staring at Honey Bunch with a very peculiar expression on his face. "You must be Honey—" he began, then stopped abruptly.

"What did you say?" Flyer Frank asked immediately.

The clerk had been frowning. Now he smiled. "I—uh—said, 'You must like honey.' I have some imported Japanese honey. Perhaps you want to buy some?"

Flyer Frank shook his head and walked over to join Honey Bunch. She was still examining the paper lantern.

Norman, in the meantime, had discovered some pottery figures on a shelf. There were three little monkeys together and Norman laughed when he saw that one monkey held its hands over its ears, another one was covering its mouth, and the third hid its eyes.

"I like these," Norman said to the clerk who had come over to him.

"Those are the famous three monkeys of Nikko," the man explained. "They illustrate the rule never to see, or hear, or speak evil."

"I know Nick," Norman observed, "but I didn't know he had any monkeys."

The clerk looked confused. "The original monkey figures are on a temple in Nikko, Japan," he told the little boy.

"Oh," said Norman with an embarrassed smile, "I was talking about my friend Nick Kito."

The man looked intently at Norman. "Where are you staying, sonny?" he asked.

"At the Shadowlawn Motel just down the street," Norman replied. "I'm bunking with Flyer Frank," he added proudly.

The shop attendant reached behind the counter and pulled out a small paper kite.

"How would you like to have this, little boy?" he remarked.

"Pollywogs!" Norman exclaimed. "That's keen! Thanks a million!"

"Where will you fly it?" the man inquired casually.

"I'll take it to the park in Barham where I live," Norman explained. "That's a good place to fly kites."

121

Norman was still admiring his gift when the clerk slipped into the room behind the shop. Suddenly the group in the shop heard a door slam, followed by the sound of running feet.

"Where did the man go?" Honey Bunch asked in surprise.

Honey Bunch and Norman dashed into the rear room. It was empty. "I wonder why he ran away?" Honey Bunch mused.

"I don't know," Norman replied. "He gave me this kite and asked me where I'd fly it. Then he left."

When the children told Mrs. Morton that the clerk had disappeared, she looked disturbed. "That's very odd," she remarked. "I think we'd better go back to the motel."

They left the shop and retraced their steps. As they walked toward the section of the building where their rooms were located, Norman cried, "Look, Flyer Frank! There's something fastened to our door!"

He and Honey Bunch ran to the room. There, tacked to the wood, was a piece of white paper. Flyer Frank was right behind the children. He snatched the paper off the door and quickly read the note.

"Listen!" he cried. "It says 'Go back to Barham and mind your own business!' "

"Who could have written it?" Mrs. Morton exclaimed.

"I don't know," the pilot replied, "but I'm going to report this to the police."

He put in the call and soon had the night officer on the line. He read the message to him.

"Oh yes, Mr. Franklin," the officer said. "I see you made a report to the captain this afternoon. I'll add this note to it. Have you any idea as to who wrote the warning?"

"Yes, but I'm not sure," the pilot replied. "I'll let you talk to Honey Bunch and Norman. They can tell you about what happened in the Oriental Shop this evening."

Honey Bunch and Norman took turns telling him about the clerk and his strange disappearance after talking to Norman.

"It does sound suspicious," the officer agreed. "We'll keep a watch on that place."

That night Norman dreamed he was hanging to the tail of a kite flying high over Barham Park. A monkey with its hands over its eyes flew by, and the kite fell.

Norman woke suddenly. To his surprise, he was lying on the floor with Flyer Frank bending over him.

"Wh-what happened?" the little boy asked, bewildered.

Flyer Frank laughed. "I guess you were dreaming. All at once you gave a great jump and flopped right out of bed."

Norman laughed, too, and climbed back into bed. Soon he was fast asleep again.

The next morning the four had breakfast early, then set out for the woods once more. This time they walked along slowly, looking up at the tops of the tall trees.

Norman put his head back so far that he suddenly lost his balance and sat down hard! When he got up, he staggered about, pretending to be dizzy.

"Norman," Honey Bunch scolded him, "you *must* be serious if you want to be a 'tective!"

Norman grinned and promised to behave. The search went on until they all had stiff necks from looking up so far. There was no sign of a broken carton or of Japanese lanterns.

Finally, when they were just about to give up, Norman gave a shout. "I see it! I see it!" he cried.

He pointed to a very tall tree whose big branches extended almost to the top. There at the end of one of the highest branches hung several paper lanterns and some scraps of tissue paper and cardboard!

"I see it! I see it!" Norman cried

"Goody!" Honey Bunch clapped her hands. "You found them, Norman!"

"But how are we going to get them down?" Mrs. Morton asked. "They're very high!"

Norman ran toward the tree. "I'll climb up and get them," he volunteered.

"Oh Norman, you can't!" Honey Bunch objected. "It's too high and you'd fall!"

"That's right, skipper," Flyer Frank agreed. "We'll have to think of some other way."

"Maybe we could go up in a balloon," Norman suggested.

Flyer Frank snapped his fingers. "Norman you've given me an idea. How about Pilot Jim and the *Merry Windmill?*"

Pilot Jim was Jim Daniels, a friend of Flyer Frank's and also of Honey Bunch's and Norman's. He flew a helicopter which he had named the *Merry Windmill.*

"How can he help?" Honey Bunch asked, puzzled.

Flyer Frank smiled. "I'm not sure if it will work, but I'm going to try! You'll see later!" he added teasingly.

The pilot suggested that Mrs. Morton and the children stay in the woods and watch the big tree. "I'll find a telephone, call Jim, and be right back," he promised.

After he hurried off, Mrs. Morton made herself comfortable at the foot of the tree. Honey Bunch and Norman thoroughly searched the ground around it.

"Maybe at least one lantern fell all the way down," Honey Bunch said hopefully. But although the children walked in a complete circle and looked under every bush they found no trace of a Japanese lantern.

It did not seem long before Flyer Frank returned. "I got Jim," the pilot told them. "I gave him the exact bearings, so he should be able to spot the tree. We'll watch for him and try to signal when he gets here."

"I can hardly wait to see what he's going to do!" Honey Bunch exclaimed, jumping first on one foot, then on the other.

"How shall we signal him, Frank?" Mrs. Morton asked.

Norman pulled a white handkerchief from the pocket of his shorts. "How about this?"

"It's awf'ly little to see from the air," Honey Bunch objected. "Tie mine to it!" She pulled her handkerchief from her pocket.

Mrs. Morton opened her handbag. "Add mine," she suggested.

Flyer Frank laughed. "I'll contribute one, too." He pulled out a large white one.

Honey Bunch found a stout stick and they tied the four handkerchiefs together and then to the end of the stick. They had just finished their job when they heard a whirring sound.

"There's Pilot Jim!" Norman shouted, pointing to a bright yellow 'copter just passing above them.

"Wave the signal!" Honey Bunch cried in excitement.

Norman grabbed the stick and waved it vigorously back and forth. The *Merry Windmill* turned and came back toward the group.

"He sees us!" Honey Bunch cried.

At this moment Pilot Jim leaned from the window and waved to them. Then he brought his craft to hover directly overhead. The wind from the spinning rotors struck the tree top and the branch bent under its force.

"I know what you mean, Flyer Frank!" Norman shouted. "Pilot Jim's going to blow the lanterns down!"

As the group watched breathlessly, the helicopter moved over until the blast from the rotors struck the end of the long branch. First several pieces of cardboard and tissue paper floated down. Then came a red lantern. In a few minutes ten lanterns had drifted down.

"Guess that's all," said Flyer Frank, looking upward at the branch.

"Thank you, Pilot Jim!" Honey Bunch cupped her hands and called as loudly as she could.

The copter pilot waved from the window again and the *Merry Windmill* churned off.

Honey Bunch ran to pick up one of the fallen lanterns. The paper was torn and some of the framework broken, but the black wooden disk at the bottom was undamaged.

The little girl held the paper globe in her hands and pressed the bottom of the frame. Then she gasped;

"Look what I've found!"

CHAPTER XII

A RUNAWAY LETTER

HONEY BUNCH held out one hand. In her palm was a string of lustrous pearls.

"Why, they're blue!" Mrs. Morton exclaimed.

Norman and Flyer Frank rushed over to examine Honey Bunch's find. The pearls were perfectly matched and of a soft gray-blue color.

"That's a most unusual shade," the pilot observed. "I've seen them in Japan, but not often in the United States."

"Let's look in the other lanterns," Norman said impatiently. "I'll bet they have pearls in them, too!"

One by one the paper lanterns were torn apart. In the false bottom of each one lay a beautiful string of gleaming pearls! Some were blue, some white, while others had a pinkish tinge.

"These are all top quality," Flyer Frank announced. "They're worth a fortune!"

130

"More than Norman's quiet gold?" Honey Bunch wanted to know.

Mrs. Morton was puzzled. "What do you mean by quiet gold, dear?" she asked.

"Mrs. Miller told me Norman had quiet gold after he broke the paper lantern," Honey Bunch explained.

"I can't think what you mean," Mrs. Morton said. "You must have misunderstood Mrs. Miller."

"I haven't any gold!" Norman insisted stubbornly.

Flyer Frank laughed. "Well, I guess that's another mystery," he observed. "But right now, we'd better report to the Wellsburg police, then head back to Barham. I'd say our work here is over."

The Wellsburg police officers were amazed to learn of the children's discovery. "We'll keep the gems here for the present," the tall captain said.

"Have you found the two bad men?" Honey Bunch asked.

"Nip Skibben and Blinky Dibert? No. I'm afraid they've run away."

"How about the man in the Oriental Shop?" Norman wanted to know.

131

"We talked to him," the captain replied. "He came right back. He said he couldn't understand why you had left. But there is something odd about him. We're keeping an eye on the place," the police officer added.

Bidding the policemen good-by, the group drove back to the garage. Flyer Frank turned in the rented car. Then the four walked to the flying field and climbed into the plane.

When they got back to Barham, Mrs. Morton thanked Flyer Frank for his help. Honey Bunch threw her arms around him. "You were just scrumptious!" she exclaimed. "Didn't we have fun?"

"We solved the paper lantern mystery," Norman said proudly.

"Only part of it, Norman," Honey Bunch reminded him. "We haven't found Nip and Blinky yet." Then she added sadly, "And we haven't had time to look for Cousin Henry for Honey Blossom."

"It won't take long to do that," Norman declared, throwing out his chest.

They waved to the pilot as he went off. Then they hurried to the Morton car. On the way home Mrs. Morton stopped to speak to Officer Reilly, who stood on the corner.

"We found lots of beautiful pearls in the paper lanterns!" Honey Bunch cried excitedly.

"Well now, did you?" the policeman exclaimed. He smiled in admiration when he heard the entire story of the successful search for the lanterns.

"You are great little detectives, Honey Bunch and Norman!" he declared. "Wait till the chief hears what you've done."

When Honey Bunch and Norman reached the Mortons' house, the little girl ran at once to the hall table where the mail usually was left. She looked through the letters, then turned away sadly.

"I haven't heard from Honey Blossom yet!" she wailed. "Maybe she never got my letter!"

"She must have received it by now," Mrs. Morton said reassuringly.

Norman, meantime, had gone home to let his mother know he was back, but in a few minutes he returned. "Let's go see Nick and Aniko," he suggested to Honey Bunch.

She agreed and the two ran down the street. Soon they were telling their Japanese friends about their adventures in Wellsburg.

When she came to the part about hearing the two men talking in the woods, Honey Bunch

133

asked the brother and sister, "One of them said your father was a nice wild duck. What did he mean?"

Aniko's little round face took on a worried expression. "It means someone who would be easy to cheat or rob," she replied. "Oh, do you think they are planning to rob Papa-san?"

"I'll warn Officer Reilly," Honey Bunch promised. "He won't let anybody steal from your father."

On her way home, Honey Bunch stopped to talk to Patrolman Reilly again. When she told him what the phrase "a nice wild duck" meant, he whistled in surprise. "I'll call the chief. He'll put a guard at The Tokyo Shop tonight. Thanks for the tip, Honey Bunch."

The next morning Honey Bunch telephoned Aniko and asked her to come over and play. "Ida is coming too," she said, "with her dolls."

When the two little girls arrived an hour later, their arms were full of dolls.

"Aniko says we can play doll festival with hers," Ida announced.

"That's fine," Honey Bunch agreed. Then she turned to the little Japanese girl. "Was anything stolen from your father's shop last night?" she asked.

Aniko shook her head. "No. Officer Reilly stopped at our house this morning. He said everything was all right at the store."

"I'm glad," Honey Bunch said. "How do we play doll festival?"

The Japanese girl explained that in her country this was a special festival held in March for girls. At this time all kinds of dolls were put on display.

"We usually take a stand with several shelves and cover it with something red. Then we place the emperor and empress dolls and all the court lady dolls on the steps. It is like a throne! It is very pretty!" she said enthusiastically.

Honey Bunch was thoughtful. "What can we use for the throne?" she mused. Suddenly her face brightened. "I know!" she cried and ran into the house.

In a few minutes she returned lugging a white flower stand. "Mother isn't using this, and she said I might take it," Honey Bunch explained.

She placed the stand on the grass, then went back into the house. This time she brought out a wide scarf of soft red wool and draped it over the plant holder.

"It is very nice," said Aniko.

She placed her dolls on the stand one by one.
Each wore a costume from ancient times. The
emperor and empress were dressed in stiff silks
embroidered in gold. The court ladies had on
ceremonial kimonos of delicate colors.

"What gorgeous dolls, Aniko!" Honey Bunch
exclaimed.

As she spoke a sudden gust of wind came up.
It toppled over the emperor and empress and
they fell to the grass.

"Oh dear!" Honey Bunch cried. "I hope
they're not broken!"

Ida quickly picked up the fallen figures. "They're all right," she said.

Honey Bunch sighed in relief. "It's getting too windy," she said. "Let's play in my room."

Aniko gathered up the dolls and Ida took the red stole. Honey Bunch carried the stand.

A little later while the girls were busy setting up the dolls again, another thought came to Honey Bunch. "What does a Japanese postman look like, Aniko?" she asked, curious.

"He doesn't look very different from yours," the Japanese girl replied. "He wears a uniform and carries the letters in a leather bag." Then she added with a giggle, "But our mailman does have to remember better than yours does!"

"What do you mean?" Ida Camp asked.

"Well, you see, in Tokyo where we lived, there are no street names and the houses don't have numbers as yours do."

"Then how does the postman know where to leave the letters?" Honey Bunch asked, puzzled.

"The city is marked off into sections," Aniko explained, "and the letters are addressed there. Then the mailman is supposed to remember where everyone in his section lives!"

137

"But what if he forgets?" Ida wanted to know.

"He can look up the name. There's a great big list which is fastened to a board at one of the main corners," the little Japanese girl replied, smiling at the others' astonishment.

"No wonder I haven't heard from Honey Blossom," Honey Bunch exclaimed. "The postman is probably still looking for her!"

At that moment the front screen door banged open and there came a shout of "Honey Bunch! Honey Bunch! Where are you?"

The little girls heard Norman storm through the house downstairs and into the kitchen. A muffled exclamation came to their ears, then silence.

"Oh dear. Something's happened to Norman!" Honey Bunch exclaimed. "Let's go see."

The three hurried downstairs and out into the kitchen. There sat the little boy on the floor. Long, curling apple peelings hung from his dark head!

"Oh Norman! You look funny!" Honey Bunch giggled. Nearby sat Mrs. Miller smiling and holding an empty bowl.

Norman grinned and looked embarrassed as he got to his feet.

"What happened?" Ida Camp asked.

Mrs. Miller explained that she had been paring apples for a pie when the little boy had burst into the kitchen. "Norman never looks where he's going," the woman said, "so he ran right into me."

"And the bowl of peelings landed on top of my head!" Norman finished the story. "I'm sorry, Mrs. Miller," he said looking up at her with serious brown eyes.

"I'm sure Norman didn't mean to do any harm," Honey Bunch assured the woman.

"Well, I'll forgive him this time," Mrs. Miller replied. She turned to a basket on the table and handed each of the children a big red apple.

"Did you want anything special, Norman?" Honey Bunch asked as she bit into the fruit.

"Pollywogs!" he exclaimed. "I forgot! The postman is coming up the street! Maybe today he has a letter from Honey Blossom!"

The children ran out onto the front porch. The mailman was just entering the Mortons' yard.

"Good morning, Honey Bunch," he called. "Where are you going in such a hurry?"

"To meet you, Mr. Postman," the little girl replied. "Is there a letter for me from Tokyo, Japan?"

"Well now, I'll have to look," the man said

teasingly. He thumbed through a handful of letters, then pulled out one.

"What do you know?" he remarked. "Here's a letter addressed to Honey Bunch Morton, Grove Street, Barham, and it has a foreign stamp on it!"

"Oh, it must be from Honey Blossom!" Honey Bunch exclaimed, eagerly reaching for the envelope.

The postman went back down the walk while the children clustered around Honey Bunch. Excitedly she tore open the envelope and drew out a thin sheet of paper. It was covered with Japanese characters!

Honey Bunch turned to Aniko. "Will you read it for me?" she asked.

The little Japanese girl nodded and stretched out her hand to take the letter. At that moment a gust of wind whisked it from Aniko's fingers and whirled it away!

"Oh, catch it!" Ida Camp screamed.

The breeze wafted the paper high in the air and it fluttered toward the street. Norman ran toward the curb, his arms extended in a desperate effort to grab the letter. It gave a final little whirl and fell to the street.

Norman was just about to step off the curb to

pick up the paper when a delivery truck came by. After it had passed, the letter was gone!

"Wh-where is it?" Norman asked in bewilderment.

"It must be stuck under the truck!" Honey Bunch cried.

CHAPTER XIII

NORMAN'S SECRET

"LET'S chase the truck," Norman urged. "Maybe your letter will fall off, Honey Bunch!"

The four children dashed along the sidewalk after the truck. They shouted to the driver, "Stop, stop!" But the cab door was closed and the man did not hear them.

Finally Norman, who was in the lead, came to a halt. "We can't catch up to the truck," he admitted, out of breath.

"It said Bondi's Food Market," Honey Bunch observed. "Let's go there. It's only two blocks more."

"All right," Norman agreed. "On the way we can look to see if the letter fell off into the street."

They searched carefully all along the truck's route. But they saw no paper with Japanese characters on it. When the children reached the market, the truck was parked in a driveway at the side of the building.

"Mr. Bondi is nice," Honey Bunch explained. "Let's ask him about my letter."

When the playmates walked into the big food store they saw a man behind the meat counter busily cutting lamb chops. He was short and plump and wore a snowy white apron.

"What can I do for you?" he asked with a jolly smile when Honey Bunch and Norman went up to the counter.

"I'd like my letter please, Mr. Bondi," Honey Bunch said politely.

"Yes, of course," the grocer replied. He put down his knife and went into a large refrigerator compartment behind him. When he returned he held out a head of lettuce to the surprised Honey Bunch. "Here you are," he said.

"No, Mr. Bondi," Norman spoke up with a grin. "She wants her Japanese letter. We think it's under your delivery truck."

"Under my truck?" Mr. Bondi looked very surprised.

"I'll show you," Honey Bunch volunteered. She and the other children led the stocky grocer to the side drive where the truck was standing.

"Your truck went by my house just as my

letter blew away," she explained carefully.
"The paper landed in the street. We couldn't
find it anywhere. So I'm sure it's stuck underneath your truck."

"I'll crawl under and look," Norman said,
dropping to his knees.

"No, no, son," Mr. Bondi protested. "You'll
get yourself dirty. I'll look."

The kindly man slowly got down on his hands
and knees. He peered under the truck.
"There's a paper of some kind stuck to the axle,"
he announced.

"That's the letter!" Norman declared triumphantly. "Can you get it, Mr. Bondi?"

"I think so." The man stretched his arm as
far as he could, but the paper was just out of
reach. With a grunt the grocer lay on his back
and wriggled under the vehicle.

All the children could see now were the man's
feet. They waited anxiously. Finally they
heard Mr. Bondi say, "I have it!"

His feet waved wildly as he tried to move out
from under the truck. But the plump grocer
could not do this.

"Oh, poor Mr. Bondi!" Honey Bunch cried,
peering under the truck. "You're stuck too!"

"I sure am!" came the sad reply.

"Don't worry," the little girl assured him. "We'll pull you out."

She motioned to the others. Then she and Aniko grasped one of the grocer's feet. Norman and Ida held the other. At a signal from Norman they all gave a mighty heave!

Honey Bunch and Aniko pulled so hard that Mr. Bondi's shoe came off. The two little girls fell back and sat down smack on the pavement!

They jumped to their feet. Again each child took hold of the man's ankles. Once more Norman gave the signal. This time when the children pulled, Mr. Bondi slid out from under the truck.

What a sight he was! His hair had gobs of grease on it, his face was red, and his once-white apron was covered with dirt.

"Are you all right, Mr. Bondi?" Honey Bunch asked. "Oh, it's all my fault."

With a great deal of puffing, the plump man put on his shoe and got to his feet. "I'm too fat to crawl under cars any more," he admitted with a rueful smile. "But there's no harm done. Here is your letter."

He handed Honey Bunch the thin paper. It was smudged, but not enough to hide the Japanese writing.

"Thank you, Mr. Bondi," Honey Bunch said gratefully. "This is a very important letter. Will you read the letter now, Aniko?"

The little Japanese girl took the paper and studied it. "I think it would be better if Mamasan reads this," she replied.

"Let's go now," Norman urged.

"Just a minute," Mr. Bondi said. "How about a little refreshment after all our hard work?" he asked jovially.

When he saw the happy gleam in Norman's eyes, Mr. Bondi led the way back into the store. He excused himself and returned in a few minutes, his face and hands washed, his hair combed, and wearing a clean white apron.

He took four bottles of cold soda-pop from the refrigerator. Then he cut four slices of liverwurst and placed them on crackers.

"Pollywogs!" Norman exclaimed as he bit into the liverwurst. "This is super!"

The children finished the tasty snack, then said good-by to the friendly grocer. They went directly to the Kitos' home. Mrs. Kito was arranging fresh flowers for the tokonoma.

"Will you please read my letter from To-kyo?" Honey Bunch asked her.

Mrs. Kito took the letter. "I will be happy to," she said with a smile. Then she translated:

"Dear Honey Bunch: My father wishes to tell Cousin Henry that there is a treasure in his *umi-neko*. Honey Blossom."

"What is an umi-neko?" Honey Bunch asked.

The Japanese woman thought for a moment than said, "I think in English you would call it a sea cat."

"A sea cat!" Norman exploded. "Does it look like a fish or a cat?"

Aniko giggled. "A sea cat is a kind of sea gull. It has a black tail and it makes a noise like a cat!"

"That sounds funny," Norman said. "I'll

look for one of those the next time I go to the seashore."

"I do not think there are any around the United States," Mrs. Kito told him, "but they are found in great numbers along the coast of Japan."

Honey Bunch was excited. "This may be a very good clue!" she said. "Let's take it to the police station!"

Norman had been thinking. Now he said, "I can't come with you, Honey Bunch. I have something important to do."

"What is it?" his playmate asked.

But Norman would not tell her. "Maybe you'll know later, but right now I'm not sure it will work," he answered mysteriously.

Ida Camp said she had to go home, but Aniko eagerly agreed to accompany Honey Bunch. Norman and Ida ran off while Honey Bunch and Aniko made their way to police headquarters.

When they arrived they found that Patrolman Reilly was in Captain Poston's office. "Go on in," the policeman at the outer desk told the little girls.

"Hello, Honey Bunch and Aniko," Officer Reilly said. "Captain Poston and I were just talking about the pearls. We haven't been able to find any trace of your bad men Nip Skibben and Blinky Dibert."

"No," Captain Poston agreed, "but one thing they have found out is that the bad men are not Japanese."

Aniko made a little bow. "My honorable parents and brother will be happy to hear that," she said gravely.

In the meantime Norman Clark was passing Elmer Gray's house. The little boy was bouncing a ball on the sidewalk.

Norman stopped. "Would you like to help me do something?" he asked Elmer.

The boy nodded eagerly.

"Then come with me," Norman said. Elmer dropped the ball and followed his friend. When they reached the Clarks' house Norman ran down the outside steps to the basement.

In a few minutes he called to Elmer. "Come down and help me carry this up."

Elmer joined Norman who was trying to drag an old metal wash tub up the cellar stairs. Together the two boys managed to set the tub on the grass near the house.

"Now we'll fill it with water," Norman said. The garden hose had been left attached to the outside faucet. Norman turned on the water and it began to pour into the old tub.

"What are you going to do?" Elmer asked wonderingly. "Sail a boat?"

"No. You'll see!" Norman ran into the house and returned with a box of salt. "Pour this in the tub while I get something else," he directed Elmer.

Norman dashed into the house again. This time when he came out he carried a square tin box.

"What's in there?" Elmer asked curiously.

"Oh, just some things I like to save," Norman answered.

He sat down on the grass and began to rummage through the box. He took out a fishing line which had been wound around a stick of wood. Next came three corks of different sizes, then a handful of bottle caps and a roll of adhesive tape.

Norman piled these things on the ground beside him. "Look at this!" he said proudly, holding up a dried starfish. "I found it on the beach last summer."

Elmer looked at it admiringly. "Shall I put it in the water?" he asked.

"No, I'll put it back!" Norman exclaimed.

"I'm looking for something else." He poked his finger around the odds and ends left in the bottom of the box.

"Here they are!" he cried in a relieved tone. "I was afraid I'd lost 'em!" He pulled out two wings of black-and-white bird feathers.

"They're wings from Honey Bunch's Japanese toy bird!" Elmer exclaimed.

Norman nodded and carefully laid them down by the side of the tub.

"What are you going to do with those?" Elmer wanted to know.

Norman did not reply. Instead he ran toward the fence separating his back yard from the Mortons'. "Come on! Help me find Lady Clare!" he called.

He boosted Elmer over the fence, then followed. The two boys looked around the yard. There was no sign of Honey Bunch's big black cat.

"Wh—?" Elmer began.

"Ssh!" Norman whispered. "I don't want Mrs. Miller to hear us."

Stealthily the boys crept around the edge of the lawn, peering under the shrubbery. Lady Clare was not there.

Then Elmer saw something under a bush near

the driveway. He ran over. Lady Clare lay sound asleep, her pink nose resting on a fallen leaf.

"I have her!" Elmer cried, picking up the animal.

"Bring her along!" Norman ordered. Quickly he climbed to the top of the fence, then held the cat while Elmer scrambled over.

In the meantime Honey Bunch and Aniko had left police headquarters after telling Officer Reilly about Honey Blossom's letter. They walked along the sidewalk hand in hand.

"We'll have to think of some way to find Honey Blossom's Cousin Henry," Honey Bunch said earnestly.

Aniko bobbed her head in agreement. "I do not understand why this honorable cousin is carrying around an umi-neko," she said with a puzzled look. "Or how there could be a treasure inside a sea gull. It is very necessary that we find Cousin Henry!"

"I'll ask Mother and Daddy how we can do it," Honey Bunch said as they reached the Mortons' house. "Thanks for coming to the police station with me, Aniko. I'll see you tomorrow."

Honey Bunch waved good-by to her little

Japanese friend and ran into the house. "Mother! Mother!" she called.

"Your mother hasn't come home yet," Mrs. Miller replied from the kitchen.

Honey Bunch joined her. "Have you seen Norman?" she asked.

"He was out in the yard a few minutes ago with Elmer Gray," the woman replied.

At that moment they heard a great shout from the Clarks' back yard. This was followed by an anguished me-ow-rrr!

Honey Bunch dashed out of the kitchen and around the corner into Norman's yard. There she halted aghast at what she saw!

CHAPTER XIV

THE MYSTERY BEARD

"NORMAN!" screamed Honey Bunch. "What are you doing to my cat?"

Poor Lady Clare, the paper bird's wings taped to her back, was splashing desperately in the tub of water!

Norman looked sheepish as he explained that he was trying to make Lady Clare into a sea cat. At this moment the bedraggled animal gave a great leap from the edge of the tub and landed in a nearby tree.

"See! Lady Clare's flying!" Norman cried in delight.

"Norman!" Honey Bunch scolded. "You know cats don't like water!"

"I'm sorry, Honey Bunch," her playmate replied. "But Lady Clare isn't hurt."

The little girl called gently to her pet. Finally the cat climbed down the tree. Honey

Bunch picked her up and carefully pulled off the paper wings.

"We'll go home, Lady Clare," she said soothingly. "I won't tease you."

Norman looked sad as Honey Bunch walked out of the yard with Lady Clare in her arms. By the time the little girl had reached her own yard, Norman was seated on the fence.

"Hi, Honey Bunch!" he called. "Please let me come over and play with you. No more sea cats, I promise."

Honey Bunch could not help giggling. "Yes, come on," she agreed, and ran to put Lady Clare in the house.

When she came back, Norman jumped to the ground. "Did Officer Reilly know anything about Honey Blossom's Cousin Henry?" he asked.

"No," Honey Bunch replied, "and they haven't found Nip and Blinky."

"Do you think we can find Honey Blossom's cousin?" Norman asked.

"Oh, we must!" she answered. "We have to tell him about the treasure!"

"I'd like to look at her letter again. I don't see how Mrs. Kito could read all those funny drawings," Norman said.

"Let's go in the house," the little girl suggested. "I'll show it to you."

The children walked into the living room. The Japanese goldfish which Honey Bunch had bought in Mr. Kito's Tokyo Shop was swimming around in its bowl on a table.

Lady Clare sat as close to the bowl as she could get. As the fish swam around, the cat's eyes followed it intently. Just as Honey Bunch and Norman came in, Lady Clare put a paw into the water.

"Lady Clare!" Norman shouted. "Leave that fish alone!"

The startled cat leaped from the table and dashed out into the kitchen. Norman and Honey Bunch followed. "I think she's hungry," Norman decided. "May I give her some of this milk?" An opened bottle stood on the kitchen table.

When Honey Bunch nodded, Norman poured a little milk into a saucer and put it on the floor. Lady Clare quickly lapped it up. Then she came to rub against Norman's leg, purring loudly.

"See!" Norman exclaimed triumphantly, "she's not mad at me any more!"

The children looked at Honey Blossom's letter, but they could not figure out anything from it. Norman went home.

That evening at the dinner table Honey Bunch told her mother and father about the letter from Honey Blossom. "Cousin Henry's treasure is in a sea gull!" she finished.

"I don't think it can be a live bird," Mrs. Morton remarked. "I've heard that gulls don't get along very well in captivity."

"Then maybe it's a stuffed one," Honey Bunch guessed.

"I have a suggestion," Mr. Morton said.

"What is it, Daddy?"

"I'm sure there are newspapers published in the United States in the Japanese language. You could put an ad in several of them."

"You mean Cousin Henry would read it and come to see us?" Honey Bunch asked in excitement. "That's a scrumptious idea, Daddy!"

Just then they heard the police-dog puppy, Mr. Reilly, barking in front of the house. Honey Bunch ran to the door to see Officer Reilly stepping from a car. He stooped to pat his namesake affectionately.

"Hello, Mr. Reilly!" Honey Bunch called to her friend. "Have you heard from Cousin Henry?"

The policeman smiled as he took off his cap. "No, I'm afraid not," he replied. "But we do have some news about the Oriental Shop in Wellsburg."

Mr. Morton came to the door. "Good evening, Officer," he said. "Come in and tell us about it."

After the patrolman had seated himself in the living room with Honey Bunch and her parents, he began his story. He said that the Wellsburg police had reported to Captain Poston.

"They suspected that Nip Skibben and Blinky Dibert had some connection with the Oriental Shop. A couple of detectives went around there and found the place deserted. The back door was open, so they went in."

"What did they find?" Honey Bunch asked breathlessly.

"They discovered that the safe was open and empty. On it were fingerprints which matched those of Skibben and Dibert on file at the police station," Officer Reilly replied.

"Do the Wellsburg police think Skibben and Dibert robbed the shop?" Mr. Morton inquired.

Patrolman Reilly shook his head. "No. It's thought that the Oriental Shop was used as a place to get rid of the Japanese pearls dishonestly," he said. "That is, the clerk there would sell them as soon as Blinky and Nip got them into this country."

"Where do you suppose those bad men have gone?" Honey Bunch asked anxiously.

"The Wellsburg police have reason to believe they've managed to slip out of the United States and are on their way back to Japan," Officer Reilly replied.

Honey Bunch looked doubtful. "I'm afraid they're going to rob Mr. Kito's shop. Remember they said he was a wild duck!"

As he rose to leave, Patrolman Reilly assured the little girl that the policeman assigned to keep special watch on The Tokyo Shop would report anything suspicious.

The following Monday morning, Norman came over to play with Honey Bunch. He had been away on Sunday to see his grandmother. The little girl told him about Officer Reilly's call at the house.

"Yippee!" Norman exclaimed. "I wish those bad men had come into the Oriental Shop while we were there! I'd have caught 'em!"

Honey Bunch giggled. "Well, maybe you'll have a chance if they come to Barham to rob Mr. Kito's shop."

"I'll get them all right!" the little boy promised, clenching his fist and looking determined.

"Daddy told me a way to find Cousin Henry," Honey Bunch remarked.

"He did? How?"

Honey Bunch explained about putting an ad in Japanese language newspapers.

"I don't know of any Japanese newspapers," Norman objected. "Do you?"

"No," Honey Bunch admitted, "but whenever Mother wants to find out anything she asks Miss Putnam at the library."

"Okay," Norman agreed. "Let's go see her."

The Barham library was on the next block. Honey Bunch and Norman often went there to take out story books or attend some of the children's entertainments.

When they walked into the cool, quiet building, they were welcomed by the librarian. Miss Putnam was a small, plump woman with twinkling brown eyes.

"What book would you like today?" she asked.

"We want a Japanese newspaper," Norman declared.

The librarian looked surprised. Honey Bunch explained about the ad which they wished to place in a Japanese paper.

"Well, let's see," Miss Putnam mused. She took down a directory and after some searching, wrote on a piece of paper the names of three newspapers. One was published in New York, the second in Chicago, and the third in San Francisco.

"Oh thank you, Miss Putnam," Honey Bunch cried.

As the children walked out of the library, Honey Bunch said, "Let's go ask Mrs. Kito to write our ad in Japanese."

When they reached the Kitos' home, Honey Bunch and Norman found Aniko and Nikkio playing in the front yard. Honey Bunch explained their errand.

"Please come in," Aniko said. "Mama-san will be most happy to help you."

Mrs. Kito greeted the children smilingly. She gave them a pad of paper and a pencil. They kneeled at a low table to write their message. After a great deal of thought and many changes, the ad read:

"Cousin Henry Yakura: Honey Blossom has a secret message for you. Please write or phone or come to see Honey Bunch Morton on Grove Street, Barham."

The Japanese woman translated it into Japanese characters and carefully made three copies. Honey Bunch and Norman thanked her, said good-by to the Kitos, and ran back to the Mortons' house.

"Mother!" Honey Bunch cried, dashing into the living room where Mrs. Morton sat at her desk, "we have our Japanese ad! May we have three envelopes and some stamps?"

"Of course, dear. Here they are." Mrs. Morton produced the supplies and admired the neat Japanese characters on the pieces of paper.

Carefully Honey Bunch put the ads into the envelopes and her mother addressed them. Norman sealed them and placed the stamps in the right-hand corner. Then the children ran out to drop the letters in the mail box on the corner.

"Oh, I hope Cousin Henry sees the notice!" Honey Bunch exclaimed. "I want him to find his treasure, don't you?"

"You bet."

At Mrs. Morton's invitation, Norman stayed to lunch with Honey Bunch. Shortly after they had eaten one of Mrs. Miller's fluffy omelets, the telephone rang. It was Aniko calling Honey Bunch.

She answered it, then returned to the dining room. She was beaming with delight. "Aniko's daddy is having a special treat at his shop this afternoon," she explained, "and he wants Norman and me to help. May we, Mother?"

"You may, Honey Bunch. But Norman must run home and ask his mother."

Norman excused himself. He dashed out the back door and over the fence. In a few minutes he was back, saying that Mrs. Clark had given permission for him to go to The Tokyo Shop.

"I'm so glad you came!" Aniko exclaimed as the two children walked into the shop a little later.

"I love special treats!" Honey Bunch cried. "What can we do?"

Aniko explained that her father had decided to hand out favors to all the customers who came into the shop that afternoon.

"Each lady will get a fan like this." Aniko picked up a paper fan and unfolded it. Pictured on the fan was a Japanese garden. There was a tiny bridge over a curving stream and a tree covered with pink blossoms.

"How pretty!" Honey Bunch exclaimed.

"What do the men and little boys get?" Norman wanted to know.

Nikkio answered by putting two boxes on a counter. "In here are gifts for the men," he announced. From one box he lifted out a key chain. From the end of it dangled a charm with a picture of Mount Fuji.

The second box was full of bamboo birds which were really whistles. Nikkio explained that these were to be given to the boys.

"They're keen!" Norman observed. "May I have one, too?"

When Mr. Kito nodded, Norman put a whistle to his lips and blew a loud blast!

"Are these for the little girls?" Honey Bunch asked when she saw a box containing tiny paper parasols.

"Yes," Aniko said. She explained that they were either for dolls or just for decoration. It was decided that Honey Bunch would hand out the favors for the little boys and the men. Norman would give the parasols to the girls and the fans to the women.

"I'd rather give out the whistles," Norman objected. "I'll look silly with those toy parasols."

"All right, Norman," Honey Bunch agreed. "I'll trade you the whistles for the parasols, but you'll still have to give out the fans."

She and Norman agreed. They took their places on each side of the door. There had been an announcement of the formal opening of The Tokyo Shop in the Barham newspaper, so there was an almost steady stream of visitors coming in.

Then for a few minutes no customers entered. Honey Bunch happened to glance across the street. Leaning against a tree trunk was an old man. He had a tangled beard and his clothes were shabby. He looked intently at the shop.

"See that man?" Honey Bunch whispered to Norman.

The little boy followed her glance. "Yes. Why?"

"I think I've seen him before. He keeps looking over here."

More visitors arrived at that moment. For a little while the children were kept very busy handing out the favors. Then during another lull, Honey Bunch gave a little squeal.

"What's the matter?" Norman asked, staring at her in surprise.

"I know the person he looks like!" Honey Bunch cried.

"Who?"

"That man with the beard. He's the one who waited on us in the Oriental Shop in Wellsburg! I think he's watching Mr. Kito's store!"

"He doesn't look anything like the man who gave me the kite," Norman protested.

"He's wearing a pretend beard," Honey Bunch replied. "If I could only hear his voice, I'd be sure."

Suddenly a thought came to her. "I know what I'll do!" she cried.

Before Norman could say a word, Honey Bunch had raced across the street. She walked up to the bearded man. "Would you like one of our favors?" she asked.

"Go away!" the man said rudely. "I don't want any."

The little girl hurried back across the street and into the shop. "I'm sure that's the Wellsburg man!" she whispered to Norman.

Honey Bunch then went up to Mr. Kito who was standing in the rear of the shop. She told him her suspicions. "I'll call the police," he said.

Mr. Kito made the call and shortly afterward a car stopped in front of the shop. Two detectives got out.

"Where is the fellow?" one of them asked Honey Bunch who ran to meet them.

"Over under that tree." She pointed across the street. To her dismay, no one was there! "Oh, he's gone! But I know it was the man from the Oriental Shop!" the little girl insisted.

"Too bad we missed him," the policeman said, "but we'll put a double guard here tonight in case he's planning any funny business!"

When Honey Bunch arrived home she learned that Mr. Morton would not be in until long after suppertime.

"Oh Mother," the little girl wailed, "I wanted to tell him about everything that happened to-day!"

"You may stay up a little later tonight, dear." Mrs. Morton smiled.

So Honey Bunch had a chance to tell her father all about the events of the day when he came home. "And I hope Cousin Henry sees the ad!" she finished, almost out of breath.

"I hope so, too," Mr. Morton replied, patting his daughter's yellow curls. "But now you'd better get to bed."

At that moment the telephone rang. Mr. Morton answered it. Honey Bunch and her mother saw a surprised expression come over his face as he listened.

"Thanks very much for letting me know, Officer Reilly," he said before replacing the receiver.

"What is it, Daddy?" Honey Bunch asked eagerly.

"The police surprised three men breaking into Mr. Kito's store just now. They nabbed two of them. One was Nip Skibben and the other *was* the clerk from Wellsburg. You were right, Honey Bunch. His beard and clothes were a disguise."

"What happened to the third man, David?" Mrs. Morton asked.

"The police are sure he is Blinky Dibert. Unfortunately he got away. The last they saw of him, he was running in this direction."

"Daddy, we must catch him!" Honey Bunch cried, racing toward the front door.

CHAPTER XV

THE JAPANESE TREASURE

"HONEY BUNCH! Come back!" Mrs. Morton called. "You mustn't go outside!"

"Please, Mother! We must catch the bad pearl man!" the little girl pleaded.

Mrs. Morton looked at her husband questioningly. He grabbed a flashlight and headed for the door. "Let her come along, Edith, but she must not leave the yard."

Honey Bunch promised and the three went out into the darkness. In the distance they could hear the wailing of police sirens.

Woof! Woof! Mr. Reilly ran out of his little dog house beside the garage. He came up to Honey Bunch and barked again as if to ask, "What's all the noise about?"

At that moment a small, touseled-haired head popped out of a window in the Clarks' house. "What's going on, Honey Bunch?" Norman shouted.

"Blinky got away from the police! He's

coming this way!" his playmate called back.

"I'll be right down!" Norman cried.

A few minutes later he and his parents hurried around the corner to join the Mortons in front of their house.

While the grownups were talking Norman drew Honey Bunch aside. "I don't think Blinky is going to run up the street," he whispered. "He'll probably try to sneak behind our houses."

"I think so, too," said Honey Bunch.

Norman went on, "Let's go look in the back yard!"

The two children left the grownups chatting on the sidewalk and quietly slipped around the house. The moon had come up and the trees cast waving shadows on the grass.

Mr. Reilly had followed the children and now thrust his wet cool nose into Honey Bunch's hand.

Suddenly Norman gripped the little girl's arm. "Look down there," he whispered. "A thin man just jumped over a hedge into the yard next to yours. Come on!"

"I can't," Honey Bunch objected. "I promised Daddy I wouldn't leave the yard! What'll we do?"

"Let's send Mr. Reilly! He's a police dog!" Norman urged.

"All right," Honey Bunch agreed.

Norman took hold of Mr. Reilly's collar and faced the puppy in the direction of the fleeing man. "Get him!" Norman hissed. "Get Blinky!"

Quick as a flash the puppy was off! He dashed across to the neighboring yard and in a second had the fugitive's trouser cuff in his teeth. The man tried furiously to shake the puppy loose, but Mr. Reilly held on, growling fiercely.

"Good boy!" Norman called. "Hold him!"

The children yelled loudly to the grownups to come. As soon as they saw what had happened, Mr. Morton and Mr. Clark ran to Mr. Reilly's assistance.

At the same time Officer Reilly and another policeman came hurrying into the yard. In a moment they were holding onto the prisoner tightly.

"Honey Bunch and Norman, is this the man who questioned you about the Japanese family?" Patrolman Reilly asked.

"Yes," Honey Bunch answered. "And we saw his picture in your police station!"

"It's Blinky all right!" Norman declared.

"This is the first time I've been caught by a couple of kids," the captured man said angrily. "I'd still have those pearls if these two hadn't been so smart!"

"Thanks to Honey Bunch and Norman," Officer Reilly said, "we'll have all three of you lawbreakers in jail. Come along!"

As Blinky Dibert was led away, Honey Bunch exclaimed, "Wasn't that tingly? Now we have only one mystery to solve—to find Honey Blossom's Cousin Henry!"

"You can work on that tomorrow," Mrs. Morton said. "Right now it's bed-time, little detectives!"

The next morning when Honey Bunch came to the breakfast table her father held out the morning newspaper.

"You and Norman are the talk of the town," he said teasingly.

Honey Bunch took the paper. Spread across the top of the first page was the headline:

CHILDREN FOOL PEARL SMUGGLERS!

Underneath was the story of how Honey Bunch and Norman had helped to solve the mystery of the paper lanterns. It also men-

173

tioned that Officer Reilly would receive a medal for his work on the case.

"I wonder if Officer Reilly is going to turn into a detective now," Honey Bunch said. "I think I'll get Norman. We'll go down to the corner and find out."

After breakfast the little girl ran into the back yard. Norman was already climbing over the fence. He had seen the newspaper too and was very excited. He agreed immediately to go with Honey Bunch and talk to Officer Reilly.

Their friend was busy directing traffic when the children arrived at the intersection. He waved to them. Then, seeing there were no cars coming for a few moments, he walked over.

"Good morning, Mr. Reilly," Honey Bunch said. "Are you going to be a detective?"

The kindly policeman smiled. "How could I leave you? Why, you children might have to run down to this corner and have me help you with another mystery! Captain Poston told me I could have the promotion to detective, but I decided I'd rather keep my job on this corner and direct traffic."

"We're glad," Norman remarked. "We'd miss you, wouldn't we, Honey Bunch?"

The little girl nodded vigorously. "May we see your medal, Mr. Reilly?" she asked.

A broad smile came over the policeman's face as he pulled a small leather case from his pocket. "Isn't that a beauty?" he asked proudly, opening the box and displaying the bronze medal.

"Pollywogs!" Norman exclaimed. "That's great!"

The officer smiled and walked back to his post. "Let's go to the Kitos' and see if they've heard everything," Honey Bunch proposed.

Aniko and Nikkio and their parents were delighted that everything had turned out so well. They also said the new business was going very well.

For the next few days Honey Bunch ran to meet the postman each morning. But there was no reply to the ad the children had sent to the Japanese newspapers.

Then late the next Saturday afternoon, when Honey Bunch and Norman were working a jigsaw puzzle in the Mortons' living room, the front doorbell rang. Mrs. Miller was busy in the kitchen, and Mr. and Mrs. Morton were upstairs, so the little girl ran to the door.

A young Japanese man stood there. He was short and slender and had a pleasant smile.

"Is this where Honey Bunch Morton lives?" he asked in perfect English.

"I'm Honey Bunch. Oh! Are you Cousin Henry?" the little girl asked, her face lighting up.

The man bowed. "I am Henry Yakura and Honey Yakura is my cousin. I saw in the New York newspaper that you have a message from her for me."

"Please come in. I'll show you her letter," Honey Bunch replied.

When Cousin Henry was seated in the living room, Honey Bunch ran upstairs and told her parents. She got the Japanese letter, and all the Mortons came downstairs. After Mr. Yakura had introduced himself again, he read the letter. Then he looked up in surprise.

"A treasure in my sea cat!" the Japanese exclaimed. "I never would have guessed it!"

Norman could keep silent no longer. "Is your sea cat alive?" he asked.

Mr. Yakura laughed. "No. It is a stuffed one which I played with when I was your age. My grandfather gave it to me."

"You still have it?" Norman asked in amazement.

Cousin Henry nodded. "Yes. Japanese children are taught to be careful with their toys. I was very proud of my sea cat. It is the only thing from my childhood days which I brought to this country. I consider it a sort of good-luck piece."

Norman spoke up, "I think I'll always keep my dried starfish."

"Is your stuffed sea cat here in Barham with you?" Honey Bunch asked breathlessly.

Henry Yakura said it was in his luggage at the motel where he was staying. "Would you like me to bring it here and open it?"

"Oh, yes!" cried Honey Bunch, relieved. She had been worried that Cousin Henry would open the sea cat alone. Then she and Norman might never know what the treasure was!

Cousin Henry left, promising to return in an hour. Presently Mrs. Morton said, "Why not ask the Kito family to come here since Honey Blossom's first note came to them?"

"Oh yes!" Honey Bunch exclaimed, and dashed to the telephone.

Soon she returned to report that Mr. and Mrs. Kito, Aniko, and Nikkio would be delighted to meet Henry Yakura. They arrived at the same time as the young Japanese.

"May I look at your sea cat?" Norman requested impatiently.

In reply Mr. Yakura placed a small bag on

the table. He opened it and took out the stuffed bird.

"Yes," Mr. Kito commented, "that is an umi-neko."

Cousin Henry turned the bird over and over in his hands. "I do not see where the treasure can be," he said in a disappointed tone.

One by one the people in the room examined the bird. Honey Bunch was the last to do so. She pulled the legs and squeezed the sides, but nothing happened. Finally she pressed one of

the beady little glass eyes. Instantly a little door in the bird's side popped open!

"Cousin Henry!" Honey Bunch squealed. "I found it!"

The young man took the toy. "There's something inside!" he exclaimed, reaching in. He drew out a small package.

Everyone crowded around. Cousin Henry pulled away the wrapping of soft padded paper. Inside was a jade statuette of an old man dressed in a long robe. He was leaning on a staff. It had been carved from a beautiful blue shiny stone.

"Blue jade!" Henry Yakura cried. "This is very valuable!"

"There's something else!" Norman cried. He had picked up the bird, and was feeling around the inside. Now he pulled out a small scroll. It was covered with tiny Japanese writing.

Henry took the scroll from the little boy. "It's a message from my grandfather!" he said, his voice trembling with emotion. "He says this little figure is my inheritance from him. It has been in our family for many, many years."

Mr. Kito took the jade statue and ran his fingers over it. "It is indeed rare and precious."

Henry Yakura took Honey Bunch's hand in his. "How can I ever thank you for what you've done?" he said. "I had not heard from my family since I came to the United States because I have moved around so much I never could give them an address. They might never have found me if it hadn't been for you! And I know Norman helped!"

"We're so glad, Cousin Henry," said Honey Bunch. "I'm going to write Honey Blossom and tell her all about it!"

Mr. Kito and his wife had been whispering together. Now he cleared his throat. "My family and I would like to entertain you all in honor of this very happy occasion. If you will accept our invitation we will have dinner for you tomorrow evening."

"Oh please come!" Aniko and Nikkio said.

Mr. and Mrs. Morton and Cousin Henry smilingly accepted. It was agreed that they would meet at the Kitos' home at six o'clock.

When the guests entered the Japanese home they gasped in pleasure. Every room was hung with gaily printed paper lanterns!

Mr. and Mrs. Kito, Aniko, and Nikkio were dressed in Japanese kimonos. Mr. Kito's robe

180

was dark gray while his wife's was navy blue with small white flowers embroidered on it. Aniko and Nikkio both wore bright red kimonos with green birds printed on them.

The four stood in a line and bowed low as the others came into the room. Then Mrs. Kito indicated that they were to take their places on cushions placed around a low round table.

"I will cook you sukiyaki," she explained. She indicated a skillet on an electric grill at one side of the table.

As the company watched, Mrs. Kito fried thin slices of beef in the skillet, then added fresh vegetables and cooked them lightly. As everyone ate it, the guests declared they had never tasted anything so delicious.

"It is our best-known dish," Mr. Kito remarked, "but all Japanese cooking is famous for its delicate flavor."

When they had finished eating, Mr. Kito raised his tea cup. "I propose a toast to Honey Bunch and Norman," he said, "who solved the mystery of the paper lantern!"

"And also the mystery of the umi-neko!" Cousin Henry added.

Everyone cheered and Honey Bunch and

181

Norman grinned in delight. Then Mrs. Morton said, "But there's still one mystery which hasn't been solved!"

"What's that?" Honey Bunch asked.

"Norman's quiet gold," her mother replied with a smile. "What is it?"

Honey Bunch laughed. "I asked Mrs. Miller this afternoon what she really said when Norman hid the broken lantern."

"Tell us," Norman demanded.

"She said, 'Silence is golden,'" Honey Bunch repeated carefully.

As everyone laughed, Norman ran to a corner and picked up a *sanisen,* a banjo-like instrument with three strings. He tried to play his favorite tune of Chopsticks on it. "I'm not silent any more!" he shouted.